## Pamela Branch and The Murder Room

>>> This title is part of The Murder Room, our series dedicated to making available out-of-print or hard-to-find titles by classic crime writers.

Crime fiction has always held up a mirror to society. The Victorians were fascinated by sensational murder and the emerging science of detection; now we are obsessed with the forensic detail of violent death. And no other genre has so captivated and enthralled readers.

Vast troves of classic crime writing have for a long time been unavailable to all but the most dedicated frequenters of second-hand bookshops. The advent of digital publishing means that we are now able to bring you the backlists of a huge range of titles by classic and contemporary crime writers, some of which have been out of print for decades.

From the genteel amateur private eyes of the Golden Age and the femmes fatales of pulp fiction, to the morally ambiguous hard-boiled detectives of mid twentieth-century America and their descendants who walk our twenty-first century streets, The Murder Room has it all. >>>

## The Murder Room
**Where Criminal Minds Meet**

**themurderroom.com**

T0352491

**Pamela Branch (1920–1967)**

Pamela Branch was born on a tea estate in Sri Lanka. She was educated in England, studied art in Paris, and attended the Royal Academy of Dramatic Art in London. Returning to the East, she lived for three years on a houseboat in Kashmir, and travelled extensively in Europe, India and the Middle East. According to her more famous contemporary Christianna Brand, she was 'the funniest lady you ever knew'; she adored practical jokes, of which she had a seemingly endless store, and the contemporary press lavishly praised her wit. The *Sunday Times* stated that 'even the bodies manage to be ghoulishly diverting' and the *Times Literary Supplement* compared her third novel, *Murder Every Monday*, to the work of Evelyn Waugh. She married twice, was, according to her friends, entertaining, glamorous, beautiful and charming, and the greatest mystery of her work is why it has not received more recognition since her untimely death from cancer at the age of forty-seven.

*By Pamela Branch*

The Wooden Overcoat
Lion in the Cellar
Murder Every Monday
Murder's Little Sister

# Lion in the Cellar

## Pamela Branch

An Orion book

Copyright © David Higham Associates 1951

The right of Pamela Branch to be identified as the author of this work has been asserted in accordance with the Copyright, Designs and Patents Act 1988.

This edition published by
The Orion Publishing Group Ltd
Orion House
5 Upper St Martin's Lane
London WC2H 9EA

An Hachette UK company
A CIP catalogue record for this book is available from the British Library

ISBN 978 1 4719 1228 3

All characters and events in this publication are fictitious and any resemblance to real people, living or dead, is purely coincidental.

No part of this publication may be reproduced, stored in a retrieval system or transmitted in any form or by any means without the prior permission in writing of the publisher, nor be otherwise circulated in any form of binding or cover other than that in which it is published without a similar condition, including this condition, being imposed on the subsequent purchaser.

www.orionbooks.co.uk

For Lynn Blair

For Lynn Eber?

# Cast of Characters

**George Heap.** The Silk Scarf Strangler, a distinguished gent who cannot endure the sight of blood. He comes from a long line of notorious murderers.

**Sukie Chandor.** George's niece and an easy target for blackmailers. Her mother was an axe murderess who is enshrined in Madame Tussaud's.

**Hugh Chandor.** Sukie's husband, who is studying to be a barrister. He and Sukie live across the back wall from the Carp.

**Mrs. Filby.** Proprietress of the Carp, a public house where all the neighborhood regularly gathers. She runs a tight ship, or tries to.

**Mr. Tooley.** The bartender, who is perpetually inebriated from stealing his customers' drinks. He has a phantom marmoset attached to his neck.

**Beecher.** A loathsome man who burgles for revenge. He has a group of henchmen who look up to him—Solly, Lights, and the Queue.

**Alistair Starke.** A bearded, unwashed young painter who lives next to the Carp and always manages to get someone to buy his drinks for him.

**Miles Tate-Grahame**. An inventor so boring even he has long since lost interest in himself. Another regular at the Carp.

**Mr. Scales.** A jolly undertaker who also lives next door to the Carp.

**Mr. Bentley.** A veterinary surgeon and infrequent visitor to the Carp. He's a petty little fellow whom no one likes.

**Marigold Tossit.** The Chandors' glamorous next door neighbor, who has superb legs and a Protector who augments her income.

**Miss Dogtinder.** A vegetarian and herbalist who lives in a hut in Marigold's garden. She keeps a goat and a garden in the bomb site across the way.

**The Great Tabora**. A retired lion tamer who rents a room from Marigold.

**Albert Chivvers.** The local constable, whose lot is not an easy one.

**Tribling.** A fellow resident of George Heap's club, and his *bête noire*.

**D.I. Stoner.** To the end, the Silk Scarf Strangler kept him guessing.

**Senator.** Mr. Scales' glum horse, who was raised believing he was a man.

**Mossop.** Mrs. Filby's ancient cat, to whom she is devoted.

# CHAPTER 1

By the time the porter brought in the lunch editions, the story had moved from the Stop Press into the headlines. George Heap bought a paper, proceeded in his usual urbane manner into the smoking room and ordered a glass of sherry. He then lit a cigar and glanced at the front page.

The account was long and confused. On page three was a picture of the scene of the crime. Badly reproduced, slightly out of focus, the bomb site had a desolate, nightmare quality. A white arrow pointed to the spot where the body had been found. Turning to the theater list, George Heap was distracted by a picture of a bleak man in a raincoat. This was Detective Inspector Stoner, who was in charge of the case. He was holding up a scarf and pointing to it with his other hand. He looked annoyed, which was understandable. Quite apart from being obliged to pose in so idiotic an attitude, this was the third similar murder in a fortnight.

George Heap sipped his sherry. He produced a fountain pen and, with a weary smile at his own childishness, gave Detective Inspector Stoner a small mustache.

He looked around the silent room. The resident club members were sunk in their chairs. Some read, some dozed. Two played an interminable game of chess. George Heap had known them all for years. He knew which one was still brooding over last night's game of bridge, which one was pondering over what there would be for lunch, which one was thinking of nothing at all ... He sighed, unutterably bored.

He was tasting his second glass of sherry when his *bête noire* arrived and approached him from behind. Tribling, who enjoyed the feud, slapped him on the back just hard enough to spill the wine. George Heap looked up, biting his lip. He then lowered his gaze and stared at his enemy's paunch. Neither spoke. Tribling blew his nose, looked mildly over his handkerchief and, with his curious gait which was not quite a run, retired.

1

He embedded himself in an armchair and opened *The Times*. From behind it, he peered at George Heap. He was waiting to see the man mop the sherry off his impeccable waistcoat. George Heap refused to afford him this pleasure. After a while, infuriated by the spying, he got up and wandered restlessly into the hall.

It was Tuesday, the day on which he normally visited his sister in her mental home and his grandfather's effigy in Madame Tussaud's. Today, he decided to do neither. Instead, he collected his hat, coat, and cane, slid into his Buick, and headed for the public house in Chelsea where he knew that he would find the only other Heap still at large, his niece Sukie.

The fact that it was still raining depressed him further. He drove without his customary care. Turning out of King's Road, he encountered an errand boy doing some fancy riding on a bicycle. He wrenched at the wheel and by a miracle avoided a head-on collision. The boy skidded into a lamp post, fell on to the pavement, and gashed his knee. He rose immediately, shouting, but George Heap was too horrified to do more than turn away his head and cover his eyes with a well-kept hand.

He felt quite sick. He could not endure the sight of blood, he could not even bring himself to think the word. It was for this reason that he had never shed a drop of it. He dispatched his victims with a silk scarf. He was exclusively a strangler.

Mr. Tooley drew a glass of Guinness and took its temperature. It was too hot again and he concealed a smile. If the Guinness inspector called, it would mean a sharp reproof for Mrs. Filby and there were few things which made Mr. Tooley happier than seeing his superior discomfited. He did not know it, but he grunted. He was a persistent grunter, but he was deaf, and never heard himself do it. He dropped the thermometer into its case, grunted and drank the Guinness.

Mrs. Filby, the proprietress of the Carp public house, was poking a ruler down the back of a settee in the saloon bar. She changed her grip and, with a quick scoop, dug out a ration book, two halfpennies, and a tuft of horsehair. At the same time she was watching Mr. Tooley in a mirror covered with an elaborate golden design – an advertisement for a branded port long since unobtainable. She had heard the telltale grunt and knew exactly what was passing through Mr. Tooley's dilapidated old mind. Mr. Tooley knew her equally well. He looked up and their eyes met in the mirror between the letters of the word Nutty.

"Seventy-two," said Mr. Tooley shuffling, patting the Guinness barrel. He thought of adding, "An' you know why," but decided against it. He was nearly eighty, and he hated talking. He merely looked pointedly at

Mrs. Filby's ancient cat, who was, as usual, asleep on top of the barrel.

Mrs. Filby took no notice. She was devoted to Mossop and knew that the animal was only happy these days when asleep in that particular place. Moreover, she had great faith in the unique properties of Guinness and believed that her customers would, if necessary, drink it just off the boil. She looked after Mr. Tooley's bent, retreating shoulders with animosity. He was eating sen-sen cachous again and she knew exactly what that meant. Her eye raced over the levels of the bottled spirits behind the counter. They were the same as they had been when she closed up last night, which meant either that he had watered them or that he was tapping the cellar again. In all the years he had worked for her, she had caught the old dodger out only once. But that had been enough to disenchant her and she had since spoken to him as little as possible. Yet she did not want to report him to the brewers. The guerrilla malice between them gingered up the exhausting, monotonous routine of her day.

Behind the weighing machine, she found a bedraggled copy of last night's paper. The Stop Press informed her that the Silk Scarf Strangler had been at it again. The body had been found in Hammersmith, as usual on a bomb site. The Strangler was coming closer. The previous victim had met his death in Bayswater. Mrs. Filby looked nervously out of the window at the wasteland opposite. There were a lot of them in London, she comforted herself. There was no reason why the Strangler should get ideas about this one.

It was a nasty morning. The wind was driving the rain down Wharf Mews and hurling it on to the cobbles. It had rained now, with leaden November ferocity, for five days. A corner of the poster on the hoarding had soaked loose and was flapping wildly. The piece which still adhered showed a pair of long, bronzed legs and a twist of sarong; the loose corner, when it lashed itself back against the hoarding, presented the other half of Dorothy Lamour sitting under a tree in tropical sunshine. Directly below her fifteen-foot figure and only an inch over one third of her size, stood the man Beecher.

He was dwarfed by the poster, but such was his stance and build that he completely dominated it. He stood with the rain bouncing off the shoulders of his discolored Burberry, his simian arms hanging at his sides, making no attempt to take shelter. He was, Mrs. Filby knew, on the wagon, which meant that he would not touch a drop before one-thirty in the afternoons and seven in the evenings. He was now gazing at his turnip watch, waiting for it to be half past one. There was something uncanny about his immobility. He wanted a drink. He intended to have a drink. She felt that, unable to entertain two thoughts at the same time, he would have stood

3

there just the same if a tidal wave had come roaring at him out of the Thames; that when the waters finally receded, Beecher would still be standing there in exactly the same attitude, dry.

Mrs. Filby looked at him with hatred. If she had dared, she would have forbidden him to use the House; but she knew his record. When Beecher was crossed, he took his revenge immediately. His enemies became the objects of intolerable and clueless burglaries.

On the stroke of half past one, pub mean time, Beecher put away his watch and surged across the cobbles into the public bar. He stood at the counter with runnels of rain pouring off his horrible cap and ordered a pint of rough cider. Sticking out of his pocket was a sodden morning paper. Mrs. Filby noted the words STRANGLER STRIKES AG. They had been jabbed at intervals with a red chalk and she looked thoughtfully at the man's anthropoid cranium. An expert in phrenology would have been able to tell at a glance whether he was capable of throttling anybody.

She was considering her own skull in the mirror when Alistair Starke arrived. His head was quite round, like a chicken's. He lived next door to the Carp on the right, and treated the saloon bar as if it were an extension of his own premises. Until Mrs. Filby had protested, he had attended the morning session in his dressing gown. Even now, he was wearing sandals and the collar of his pajama jacket protruded from the neck of his painting smock. His feet were unclean and he had toenails like an eagle. Under his arm was a daily paper. Part of the headline read THIRD VICTIM STILL UNIDE.

Without moving his head, he looked around quickly and went straight through to the telephone in the passage to kill time until somebody, anybody, should appear from whom he could cadge a drink. Mrs. Filby opened the hatch at the back of the bar so that she could keep an eye on him. She disliked and distrusted young men who neglected to wash, wore beards, picked their noses, bit their fingernails, and painted for a living. Alistair Starke did all five. Moreover, on the rare occasions when he was obliged to buy his own drinks, he always counted his change twice. That enraged her.

Unaware that he was observed, Alistair sat down on an empty lager crate and began to scribble on the directory. He was at present under the influence of Picasso when the latter was under the influence of Matisse who had at the time been flirting with the *scuola metafisica* of Giorgio Morandi. His paintings looked like a mixed grill smeared across a menu. When he heard the door slam, he leapt to his feet with a broad smile.

The new arrival was Miles Tate-Grahame. He was hanging up his dripping mackintosh on the weighing machine and he looked even taller, grayer, and more lopsided than usual. He had an evening paper in his hand.

"Mornin'," said Mrs. Filby. "They caught the Strangler?"

"No," said Miles. He grinned sourly. "But 'An Arrest is Expected Hourly'."

"Well, amigo," said Alistair ingratiatingly, "how goes it? How fares the turbine? How does your culture grow?"

The inventor looked at him sideways, his eyes behind the thick, bifocal spectacles no bigger than dried peas and of much the same color. He was tired of keeping Alistair in beer. But the man was his neighbor and the only person in the vicinity who would listen to long, boring recitals of his scientific experiments.

"Drink?" he asked. "As if I didn't know."

Alistair thrived on insults "Thanks," he said brightly. "Bitter, please."

" 'Alf?" asked Mrs. Filby, hoping to shame him.

"Pint," said Alistair firmly. He narrowed his eyes at her.

Mrs. Filby did not like either of them. Drawing the bitter, not the best bitter which she knew that they were expecting, but the weaker one which she privately referred to as "cooking," she glanced at Miles' skull. It was covered with uneven protuberances like a rock. She shortchanged him eightpence.

The inventor did not notice. He hardly ever noticed anything. He was such a bore that even he had lost interest in himself. He drove Alistair into a corner and embarked upon one of the dull monologues to which neither Alistair nor Mrs. Filby ever bothered to listen.

When her other neighbor, Mr. Scales, bounced in, Mrs. Filby looked at his skull with admiration. It was full, rounded, and covered with soft, white hair. He was an undertaker. In choosing the site next door to the Carp, he had forfeited a certain type of customer, but he considered that it was worth it. It was very handy during the slack summer months or a winter without epidemic to wait for custom in the saloon bar. Wharf Mews was a cul-de-sac. Unless his clients swam through the A.R.P. emergency tank at the far end, they had to pass the windows of the public house. This gave Mr. Scales just time to nip over the back wall, eat a piece of parsley, which he believed had deodorant qualities, and be waiting soberly and sympathetically in his parlor when his acolyte ushered in the bereaved.

He rested his jolly paunch against the counter, mopped the rain from his cherub's face and beamed at Mrs. Filby.

"I shall take a small rum," he chirped.

Mrs. Filby nodded understandingly. Mr. Scales always fortified himself with rum before a funeral. "Anyone I know?" she asked.

"No," said Mr. Scales. "Trick rider. Wall of Death. What a mess!"

"*Requiescat in pace*," said Mrs. Filby, pouring rum.

"*Hic jacet*," said Mr. Scales automatically. "Killed two bystanders into the bargain. Macomber an' Pitt got them," he added with a trace of resentment.

"Never mind," said Mrs. Filby. "Lot o' new diseases about."

"Ar," said Mr. Scales, "but look at all these newfangled drugs. Sulphur. Imagine little old sulphur turnin' on us like that!"

"You want to get in touch with the Strangler," said Mrs. Filby.

She looked around for the tot of rum she had poured for him. It had vanished. Mr. Tooley was down at the far end of the bar eating sensen.

"There 'e goes again!" said Mrs. Filby bitterly. "You can't *prove* anythin'."

The door swung open and George Heap came in. He looked around with ill-concealed distaste. Seeing that his niece had not yet arrived, he ordered himself a small brandy and stood sipping it at the counter. Both Mrs. Filby and Mr. Scales were delighted to see him. He was the Carp's most distinguished customer. Today, however, he was clearly in one of his more taciturn moods and neither of his admirers cared to break the silence.

The next arrival was a small man in oilskins and sou'wester. He scurried in, stopped on the threshold, and shook himself very much like a terrier.

"If it isn't Mr. Bentley!" said Mrs. Filby, forcing a smile.

Mr. Scales, who had not turned round, gave her a startled glance and hurried away into a corner. Mr. Bentley was used to this sort of treatment. People always avoided him. Mrs. Filby, however, was unable to escape. She saw the little veterinary surgeon only about twice a year. He lived on the south coast but sometimes went North to put one of his farmer brother's doomed animals out of its misery. On these occasions, he stayed a night in London and always dropped into the Carp to sow a seed of dissension and pay his respects to Mrs. Filby. He had made her acquaintance a number of years ago when she had possessed a cat considerably bigger and hotter than Mossop. This animal had led her a continual dance until Mr. Bentley had nipped its nymphomaniac career in the bud. She had later learned that he was a petty little fellow, rich in malice, but the cat's metamorphosis had been so satisfactory that she had never forgotten it.

"Who was that?" asked Our Mr. Bentley. "Eh? Came in just before me? Who was it?"

Mrs. Filby looked around for George Heap. He had disappeared. She was puzzled. She concluded that he had vanished into the toilet, but he

6

must have moved with quite extraordinary speed. She looked back to Mr. Bentley. Something in his eye made her cautious.

"I dunno," she said. "Never saw 'im before. Why?"

"Eh?" said Mr. Bentley. He scratched his face. "Oh, nothing." He felt her eyes still upon him and suddenly lost his temper. "How dare you question me?" he said shrilly. "Bring me a Guinness and mind your own business!"

When Hugh Chandor turned down Wharf Mews it had stopped raining and a brisk, chill wind was already drying the cobbles. He saw that Senator, Mr. Scales' large black horse, was out on the bomb site again. That meant that there would be a funeral that afternoon. Senator was always put out before going on duty. He kicked about among the rubble and ate a lot of ferns, which Mr. Scales had found quieted him down. He saw Hugh, whinnied, and went quickly behind the poster of Dorothy Lamour.

In the far corner of the wasteland, inside a half-obliterated house, sat Miss Dogtinder. She was milking her goat.

Hugh strode across the road and into the Carp. He looked around for Sukie, his wife. His heart sank when he saw that she was sitting in a corner with Mr. Bentley. She was, like all the female Heaps, far too friendly, a bad judge of character. She would talk to anybody and she usually said too much. Conversation was apt to go to her head.

"Sukie," he said.

She jumped up, skipped over to him, and clutched his arm. Her small, freckled face was pink with excitement. She might not have seen him for a year.

"Hullo, darling," she said in her curiously light voice. "You've got a new hat. You do look pretty. You're hours and hours late."

Hugh looked at his watch. "Four minutes," he said. He always pointed out her exaggerations. He was still hoping to cure her of the habit.

"Do you know a very odd thing?" Sukie rushed on. "Mr. Bentley once bought a horse for Mummy."

Hugh started. *She's been talking again*, he thought. "Oh?" he said with just the right degree of polite disinterest. He nodded to the little vet with the shifty eyes, took Sukie's arm, and started to turn away.

"Yes," said Mr. Bentley. "Yes, indeed." He put his skinny little claws on to his knees and played a rapid scale. He had a nervous tic under the left eye. "I had a letter from Victoria only recently. Beautifully phrased, most concise."

Hugh did not answer. He hated people knowing that his mother-in-law was in a lunatic asylum. He ground his teeth and went to buy a drink.

When he came back, Mr. Bentley was waiting for him, the small eyes sparkling with spite.

"I knew Hannah, too," he said slyly.

"Granny?" asked Sukie. She sounded pleased.

Hugh looked quickly around to see whether anybody was listening. Alistair Starke was sitting on the next settee not listening to Miles Tate-Grahame and watching Mr. Bentley from under his eyebrows. Hugh stepped in between them. Hannah Heap was the skeleton in his cupboard and he did not, if he could help it, intend to have her aired in his local.

Mr. Bentley made a nervous genuflection. In the way that people grow to resemble their pets, he had become successively more and more like a fox terrier. He had been breeding them for forty-five years, all exactly alike, the descendants of an unusually dominant champion.

"As a matter of fact," said Mr. Bentley with satisfaction, "it was I who sent for the police."

Hugh stared at him. He did not know quite what to do. He wondered whether the man could be contemplating a mild form of blackmail.

"Yes, indeed," said Mr. Bentley. His left eye closed completely in a spasm of twitching, but he did not notice it. He was enjoying himself. "What a catastrophe! She was, I assure you, completely *amok*! One, I could perhaps have understood, in a moment of confusion. But five ... *no*! Carnage! I've never seen anything like it. I've often wondered what happened to the axe." He smiled at Sukie. "People around here – um – *know*, eh?"

"They will do soon", said Hugh savagely, "if you don't lower your voice."

"Ah," said Mr. Bentley. "Very wise, keep it dark, eh? No need for unpleasantness. I suppose that if it was bruited abroad, people might think, it's just possible that they might think ..." He spread his small hands. "An unfortunate family tree. What a stigma!"

"What are you driving at?" said Hugh aggressively.

Mr. Bentley looked at Sukie. "So young too!" he said, shaking his head.

Normally, Hugh was a quiet and controlled young man. When goaded, he occasionally behaved rashly. "I don't like your face," he stated.

Mr. Bentley laced his fingers together. "What a pity," he murmured. "Because you will undoubtedly see it again." His eye twitched and he gave it an impatient little slap. "Soon," he added.

Sukie glared. "I don't like you," she said. "Go on, *hump off*!"

Mr. Bentley shook his head sadly. "Hannah," he said, "Victoria, and now, my dear, *you*! A terrible handicap!" Then, well pleased with his morning's work, he snatched up his mackintosh, gave Hugh a canine grin, and darted out into the rain.

Almost immediately George Heap appeared from the passage. He was pulling on his gloves and looking thoughtful. He saw that his niece was still staring angrily after Mr. Bentley, and touched her on the shoulder. "I don't think," he said deliberately, "that he will bother you again."

"He is a scab," said Hugh with violence.

"An odious character," said George Heap. His voice was expressionless. "He has exploited our family for too long."

Sukie looked at him. His expression made her say quickly, "Uncle George, you're not to do anything rash."

George Heap smiled. "I never do anything rash," he said.

Sukie took his arm. She had complete confidence in him. "Promise?" she said.

George Heap patted her hand. "I promise," he said. He lit a cigar and looked out of the window, studying the bomb site opposite with a critical eye.

Between the saloon and the public bars, there was a cubicle about ten feet square. It was known as the Ladies', Bar. It was difficult to see, without craning, who was in there. At one time it had been used by visiting toffs who wished to drink in privacy. It was now patronized almost exclusively by three charwomen named Mae, Lil, and Doris. These three Fates were inseparable, drawn together by stubborn afflictions, which they discussed with the persistence of a Greek chorus. Mae had Feet; Lil had Veins and an incipient goiter; something secret inside Doris had slipped.

From one to two o'clock in the afternoon, from six o'clock onwards in the evening, they could be heard clearly all over the House. The progress of their evergreen ailments was therefore common knowledge to Mrs. Filby's goodwill. Seen out of the context of the Ladies' Bar, a casual observer might have mistaken the durable trio for a music-hall turn. They looked like joke hags. But they were not. Even Beecher was aware of their propensities and avoided them as certain terrifying animals will avoid others of an equally fearsome species.

Today they sat in a tipsy row on the wooden bench in their usual places and drank Moussec at two-and-ninepence a glass. It was no coincidence that they earned two-and-ninepence an hour for scrubbing out people's houses.

" 'Member Mr. Tonks?" asked Lil.

"Hurp!" barked Mae involuntarily, raising calloused fingers to her lips.

"Run over," said Lil. "Right in front o' 'is wife's eyes. Blood! You should of seen it. Splashed right inside the International!"

"You 'ave another, dear?" asked Doris. She rose and rapped a coin on the counter.

" 'Orrible month, that was," said Lil. " 'Ardly got over that 'fore young Cosey up an' shoots 'is Nell."

Mae slipped off her left shoe. "You don't say," she said.

"I do that," insisted Lil. "She wasn't took then, though. Was only the arm they 'ad to amputate. Fortnight later, it was, when Cosey was sentenced. Jumped under a train at Goodge Street. 'Er mum identified 'er by the bangle."

Mae, bored, returned to the conversation she had been enjoying half an hour ago. " 'E chased 'er right down to the Docks," she announced. "She wasn't 'alf scared. Thought it was the Strangler. Makin' like she was an 'eroine! I tell 'er straight I'd rather 'ave stranglin' any day more'n *these*." She shot a venomous glance at her feet.

Doris, returning from the bar with three Moussecs, gave an eldritch screech. The intelligence had amused her.

Lil displayed her baby goiter. "Just look at that today!" she said. "I ask yer."

"Ought to see my scar this thundery weather," said Doris complacently. "Even frightens Bert sometimes. 'E was on at me again larst night to 'ave It stitched up again, but what I says is if It's dropped, It's dropped, an' there It is."

"Where?"

"Dunno for certain. Don't show up on an X-ray."

"An' 'ow do *you* feel, dear? In yerself, I mean."

"Worse," said Mae simply.

Mr. Tooley, with the speed of a conjurer, whisked away the half-finished Moussec and loped into the passage to drink it. He grunted, swallowed noisily, popped a cachou into his mouth, grunted, came back to the bar, and washed out the glass. The whole operation had taken less than four seconds. Nobody had noticed, not even Mae. Mr. Tooley, congratulating himself upon his dexterity, dried the glass and put it carefully down on the air half an inch from the counter.

Mrs. Filby spun round, compressing her lips. As Mr. Tooley had expected, she said nothing. She would reserve her comments until early tomorrow morning when his resistance was at its lowest. He went painfully down on his knees and began to sweep up the pieces. *I got to stop it*, he thought frantically. *I got to. Can't 'ave 'em again yet, only two months from the last go.* He was haunted by the specter of delirium tremens. For

10

a moment he shut his eyes while he regained his equilibrium. The voices flowed around him.

"Packet o' Stafford Cripps." That was Beecher in the Public. Almost immediately it was followed by the animal crunch of potato crisps.

"I ought to have socked him," said Hugh Chandor.

"That would have been imprudent," said George Heap. "It is very simple. He must be ... suppressed."

A laugh. It was like Sukie Chandor. "For a moment," she said, "I thought that you were going to say something awful. It just shows how people get suspicions."

Mr. Tooley opened his eyes. *What are we comin' to?* he thought. *'Orrors an' violence! Turn it up, Tooley! You've 'ad a drop too much.*

The Carp was little frequented. It was off the beaten track and was not easy to find. The mews in which it stood was not prepossessing. The few regulars who lived in the immediate neighborhood did not welcome interlopers. The odd stranger who drifted in felt this and rarely returned. The Carp was too quiet, too drab, too respectable ever to become fashionable. It had been badly undermined during the war by the bomb which had dropped opposite. It was odd, dreary, and condemned.

Outside, it began to rain with redoubled fury. The sky sagged. A beetling black cloud spread over Hammersmith. A sudden spear of lightning killed two men and a boy in Putney. The Thames rose and gurgled only four feet below the flood level of 1926. The wind screamed through the chimneys of Kensington and tore the conductor off a 27 bus; it hurled the rain against the mullioned windows of the Carp and lashed up tiny waves in the puddles in the road. The rain churned in the gutters and flattened the weeds on the bomb site. It beat down four more bricks from the shell of a burnt-out house, and drove the sightseers away from the scene of the Strangler's latest coup. Miss Dogtinder's goat, matted and sodden, discovered that by standing on its hind legs it could just reach the bottom of the poster of Dorothy Lamour. It gripped pulpy slack with its rubbery lips and pulled gently. It detached the word Technicolor and ate it.

## CHAPTER 2

THAT evening Hugh Chandor did not jump off the bus as it passed Tite Street. He went sedately on to the official stop and walked back slowly, staring down at his feet.

He was worried. First, there was Sukie. He was nearly always worried about Sukie. Lately, her exaggerations, in spite of all his efforts, were deteriorating into downright lies. Because of her unfortunate background, Hugh viewed her slightest abnormality with foreboding. He knew that it was useless to brood over it, but her history could not have been more discouraging.

Her mother, Victoria Heap, had reacted to Hannah's homicidal brainstorm by immediately marrying her first cousin. Her friends and relatives had argued that she had no right to marry at all, but that if she insisted, the worst possible spouse she could choose was a relative. Victoria answered tartly that her mother had been sane; she had been hanged, which proved it. There was a stubborn streak in the Heaps. Opposition excited them.

Defiantly, she conceived her only child. In the same frame of mind, her husband, unable to face the confinement, cut his throat with a comb two days before Sukie was born. Friendless and outlawed by her family, the bereaved Victoria devoted herself exclusively to her sickly little offspring. Sukie could do no wrong in her mother's eyes. She developed at an early age a vivid imagination and a talent for lying which Victoria did nothing to check. The two of them lived in a trauma of make-believe.

By the time Sukie was fourteen, fantasy had become fact, reality the fairy tale. She had a rude shock on her eighteenth birthday. The world stepped in, certified Victoria, and carried her off to the nearest Home. George Heap had protested strongly at this move, but it was in fact not unreasonable. Victoria, after an alarming experience with a hayrick, had acquired a taste for arson.

In the Home, she had made frequent and invalid wills. By the last of these, she left all her real and personal estate to a minor Elizabethan poet and appointed the Aga Khan as her executor. After suitable inquisition, the Master in Lunacy revised this idiotic document in Sukie's favor. An official of the High Court was assigned to control her finances until she reached her years of discretion. This occurred two years later. She marched into the official's office and informed him that she had married a dear man whose name she had temporarily forgotten. The Heaps had fugues.

Grandma Hannah's loss of temper and the subsequent pogrom had taken place just before an electrical storm. It had unconsciously become Hugh's custom at the first rumble of thunder to switch his thoughts abruptly to his wife. Tonight, the thunder was muttering over the next borough.

That was the first, the recurrent worry. The second was Mr. Bentley. Obviously, the little animal doctor was contemplating blackmail. Hugh could, of course, go to the police, but, should Sukie's history become common knowledge, it would not help his career. He was still hoping to pass his Finals and become a barrister. Even if this time, the third time of asking, he managed to scrape through, scandal in the family was unlikely to be an asset at the Bar. He sighed heavily, changed his briefcase to the other hand, and dropped *Criminal Law in a Nutshell*.

He picked up the book and stuffed it into his pocket. Criminal law was his undoing. The other subjects, he sailed through without a qualm; but when, in the ominous silence of the examination room, he was confronted with the multiple conundrums of the felonies, the finesse of murder, the complexities of manslaughter and homicide, his mind became a maddening blank. He could not account for it but this always happened.

He suddenly realized that he was outside Miles Tate-Grahame's house which was next door to his own. He looked into the lighted window and saw the inventor in the front room with Marigold Tossit. Marigold, who liked all men and distributed her favors impartially, was sitting on the table swinging her superb legs. She wore black net stockings and patent leather pumps with four-inch heels. She must have been to the Odeon because she had done her hair like Joan Crawford and painted her mouth to match. Miles was reading aloud from a large, heavy book. Marigold was looking into her compact mirror and making her mouth tremble like Joan Crawford's during the telephone scene.

Hugh turned up his own small flagged path. Cork Street was a narrow lane parallel to Wharf Mews in which stood the Carp. The two-story cottages had originally been laborers' dwellings. But a few years ago an enterprising builder had bought the lot as an investment and allowed his imagination to run riot. He had painted them in quaint pastel shades, added bogus beams, cupolas, patios, and wrought-iron work; and he had multiplied the rent by eight.

There was a rattling peal of thunder and Hugh looked apprehensively over his shoulder. It was very dark. The street lamps cast feeble pools of light. He had the impression that the clouds were very low, just above the chimneys. The wind had dropped and there was an unpleasant breathlessness in the air. The bare trees were motionless, waiting for the storm to return.

Hugh let himself into the house. The hall was in darkness but there was a thread of light under the kitchen door. He went along the passage and turned the handle. The door was locked. Inside, something metallic was thrown into the sink.

"Sukie, open up!"

"Hullo, my love," came Sukie's voice. "I'm madly busy. You can't come in."

"Don't horse around, sweet. I'm tired and testy."

13

"Poor, poor," said his wife. "I won't be long."

"What are you doing?"

There was a slight grunt from the far side of the door. "I won't say. It's top secret." A slithering noise and a bump. "Damn!" said Sukie.

"Sukie, don't play idiot child. Let me in."

"No."

There was a sound of material tearing. Hugh began to lose his temper. All he wanted was a little peace and a double gin. Also he wanted to get into the kitchen.

"Sukie," he said loudly, "will you open this door or will I break it down?"

"You break it down."

Hugh swore softly. He had no intention of smashing his own door but his wife in such moods had to be taught a lesson. He lunged against the door halfheartedly. It held. It jarred his shoulder and sent a sharp pain down his arm. For a moment he thought he had fractured his collarbone. He lost his temper completely. He backed six paces, rushed at the door, and hurled his whole weight against it.

There was a crackle of splintering wood and a sharp report as the lock gave. The door burst in and banged against the wall. Hugh stalked into the kitchen. Then he stopped in his tracks; his mouth fell open. He clutched at the sink for support.

Sukie, her sleeves rolled up, looking busy and efficient, was trying to push a limp man into the housemaid's cupboard. His head was among the brooms and she was straining at his legs. He was either unconscious or dead.

"You shouldn't have come in," said Sukie, immediately on the offensive. "I knew you'd be angry." She dropped the man's legs.

"Who is he?" said Hugh. His voice was faint and without expression.

"It's Mr. Bentley. Isn't it *dreadful*?"

Hugh braced himself against the wall. "Is he dead?"

His wife picked up a sou'wester off the floor and threw it into the cupboard. "Yes," she said. "I think so."

Hugh moved with an effort. He picked up the limp wrist and felt for the pulse. There was none. The flesh was already cool.

"He's dead."

"How awful," said Sukie.

"What happened?"

Sukie's eyes flickered. "A man came in," she said. "He was wearing a black mask and he was very tall. He was wearing gloves and ..."

Hugh took her by the shoulders and shook her. "You're lying. Tell me the truth. What happened?"

His wife clung to his lapels. "They were wearing hoods," she said hopefully.

"*Sukie!*"

"Yes, darling?"

"You've got to tell me what happened."

"But you won't believe me. I know you won't."

Hugh said nothing. *It's happened*, he thought. He realized with horror that he felt a sort of relief. Subconsciously, he had for years been expecting something like this. Now it had happened. He knew where he stood. Sukie took the handkerchief out of his pocket and blew her nose.

"I found him," she said. "I went outside to hang up some bacon peel for the birds and I just found him. It was very dark and I didn't know who it was. I dragged him into the kitchen ..."

"Why didn't you send for a doctor?"

"Because I held a mirror near his nose and there was no fog so I knew he must be dead."

"He may have been breathing through his mouth."

"I didn't think of that."

"Why didn't you send for the police?"

"Well, there was blood on me. I thought they'd think I'd done it."

"Why should they?"

"Because," said Sukie.

"Because why?"

"Don't roar at me."

"Answer me."

"Well, because of ... well, Mummy and Granny and everything." She looked up at him sideways. "I thought perhaps," she said tentatively, "that we could palm him off on the Strangler."

"Why were you putting him in the cupboard?"

"I was going to break him to you gently. After dinner, I thought, when we were having coffee."

Hugh ran a hand through his hair. Then he saw the axe. It was lying in the sink and the head and handle were spattered with blood. "An axe," he said. "It was done with an axe."

"Yes, just like Granny's ones. That's why I thought ..." She saw her husband's face and her voice trailed away. She laced her fingers together and gave a long, shuddering sigh.

"Sukie, look at me."

She raised wide, greenish eyes.

15

"Tell me the truth. Did you do it?"

"No."

Hugh let her go and turned away. She caught his arm.

"You don't believe me," she said.

Hugh looked down at her. "No," he said slowly. "No, I don't." He walked out of the kitchen and slammed the splintered door.

Sukie sat down on the table and considered her next move. She was disappointed but not surprised by Hugh's reaction. She knew that he would not send for the police. But the sooner she got rid of Mr. Bentley, the better it would be for all three of them. She had a deep faith in the adage *Out of sight, out of mind.* Wondering whether there was some quiet nook outside where she might bury the body, she wandered into the dark garden. The builder had laid winding concrete paths, a sundial and a rockery. There was no room to bury anything human unless it were done vertically.

She lopped the head off a chrysanthemum and hung moodily over the wall. Next door, Miles Tate-Grahame was in his laboratory at the bottom of the yard. The lights were on and, against the frosted glass, Sukie saw him bending over and stirring something. Then he straightened up and came to the door. He had a retort of liquid in one hand which he emptied on the gravel. It sizzled, frothed, and evaporated in a cloud of smoke.

"Miles," called Sukie. She did not like the man, but the cheesy precipitate left by the acid gave her an idea.

Miles looked up. With the light behind him, he was enormous. One of his shoulders was slightly higher than the other.

"What?" he said sourly.

"Have you got any sulphuric acid?"

"A little. Why?"

"I think I'd need quite a lot."

"I've only got a little."

"Pity."

"Why?"

"I just wondered."

Miles did not like Sukie much either. He knew that she thought him a bore. He went back to his laboratory and roared his Bunsen burner.

Sukie leaned against the wall and thought hard. She considered ringing up George Heap and immediately decided against it. He would be shocked to the core. He would probably hand her over to the police at once. Victoria had told her that, although he adored his mother, he had shown no emotion whatever when the black flag was hoisted over Wandsworth. Victoria, of course, would take the matter in her stride, but visit-

16

ing day was not until tomorrow and Mr. Bentley had got to disappear tonight. *I am all alone*, she thought dramatically. *I have angered my husband and I have nobody to turn to, I mean to whom to turn.*

She climbed over the back wall and lowered herself into the yard of the Carp. She let herself in through the side door and went along the passage to the saloon bar to see whether there was anybody there whom she could cajole, bully, or bribe into being an accessory after the fact.

## CHAPTER 3

THE GREAT TABORA had once been rated among the four best lion tamers in Europe. Born in Paddington, he had run away from home at nineteen and, with the money he had stolen from his mother, who had stolen it from his father, he bought a cheap panther with rickets. He toiled with it for as long as his money held out, then took a job in a fourth-rate circus. By the time he was twenty-three he had the panther where he wanted it and two more as well. He neither smoked nor drank. He was not interested in women. He put his whole salary back into the business. At thirty-five, his dream came true. He bought his first lion. It was lame and blind in one eye. He called it Aurora.

Aurora was middle-aged. She had been born in captivity and was the mildest lion in the world. She would suffer any indignity for peace and quiet. She allowed the panthers to ride upon little platforms on her back, tolerated the Great Tabora's head in her mouth twice a day, leapt apathetically through the rings of fire. She was a failure at the box office. She never learned to roar.

She was wayward only once. That was in Ceylon. The Great Tabora and his elderly accomplice were in transit for Madras. Just outside Trincomalee, Aurora got her first whiff of the jungle. She was missing for three days. On the fourth she was rounded up and returned to her cage. She was more docile than ever. Eight months later she retired from public life and gave birth to one small male cub.

By the time little Roarer was eighteen months old, he was receiving an average of four fan letters a day. He was magnificent. He was intelligent, obedient, huge; and there was about him the authentic menace of the jungle which made him a star almost overnight. Soon he and Tabora topped the bill. The two of them – with two panthers, a leopard, and a jaguar as stooges – performed before the crowned heads of Europe. Tabora acquired a Rolls Royce, tested out a foreign accent, and discarded it for an American one. The years passed profitably. Then one wild day in September, a week before Roarer's fifth birthday, the famous lion lay down and fell into a sleep from which he never awoke.

The Great Tabora lost his job. He had Roarer stuffed, sold the panthers, the leopard, and the jaguar, abandoned the circus. Disdaining even to claim on the insurance policy, he vanished overnight, taking with him only his broken heart and his stuffed lion. A week later, haggard and unkempt, he rented a bed-sitting-room from Marigold Tossit, who lived next door to the Chandors. Marigold, as had five other landladies, complained at once about Roarer. He was too large to be carried up the narrow staircase and had to remain in the hall, where he frightened her every time she passed. The Great Tabora unwillingly accepted the inevitable. With tears in his eyes and rum on his breath, he approached Mr. Scales about the animal's burial.

This particular, eventful evening, with the ceremony scheduled for eleven o'clock the next morning, the undertaker was trying to comfort his client. The process was expensive. The only soothing influence proved to be large rums with Guinness for chasers.

"I loved that cat," said Tabora with mournful resonance, "like he was my own flesh and blood." Years of shouting at his troupe over the din of a brass band had made him unable to lower his voice.

" 'Ave a firkin," said Mr. Scales. "That's what you need."

"I'm all washed up," said Tabora gloomily. "Gimme a large rum."

Sukie arrived, blowing on her cold hands. She marched over to the mourners and came to the point immediately.

"Tell me, Mr. Scales," she said. "Have you ever buried anyone without a death certificate?"

Mr. Scales smiled tolerantly. She was a nice little girl, interested in everything, always asking odd questions. "No," he said. "Couldn't even get a burial order."

"You wouldn't even consider it?"

"No. Against the law." He looked at her curiously. "Why?"

"I was just wondering." Sukie nodded and wandered along the passage to the kitchen.

Mrs. Filby was in there, wrapping a red mullet in a piece of greaseproof paper. Mossop lay in a baking tin and watched restively.

"Do you like me, Mrs. Filby?" inquired Sukie.

Mrs. Filby pushed a plate across the table. " 'Ave a sausage roll," she said. "You look peaky."

"No, thank you." Sukie sat down on the table. She knew that Mrs.

18

Filby was devoted to her and would do almost anything to help her. "I have got no mother or father," she said richly. "Everybody's against me."

Mrs. Filby put the mullet into the oven, dropped a slab of cod into a saucepan and turned on the gas.

"I am an orphan," said Sukie. "An orphan and a pauper."

"No, you're not. You're not either."

"You don't like me. Nobody likes me."

Mrs. Filby wanted to get her supper finished and relieve Mr. Tooley behind the bar before the evening rush started. "Run along now," she said. "I got all sorts to do. That man Beecher's clogged the lock on the Gent's again. Ten groschen last week an' now it's eight annas."

Sukie went back to the saloon and bought herself a ginger beer. Mr. Scales and Tabora were still there. Mr. Scales was beginning to look harassed. His client was getting out of control. Sukie looked critically at the lion tamer. She awarded him two out of ten for sobriety. He had reached the stage which she privately referred to as Naughty Geyser.

"Who brought him into the world?" he was bawling. "Who fed him when his Mom spurned him? Who nursed him through the croup? Is that cat grateful? What does he do? He lifts one off the ground and whams me in the puss!"

"Well," said Sukie tactlessly, "I think he's a jolly good riddance."

Tabora's arms fell to his sides. He turned on her violently. His mouth closed with an audible click. For a moment Sukie thought that he would strike her. Then he bit his lip, laid a hand over his heart as if mortally wounded, turned on his heel, and swept unsteadily out into the night.

"Hammy," said Sukie unsympathetically. "Very, very hammy."

"You shouldn't 'ave said that," said Mr. Scales. "Only s'afternoon we nailed up Roarer."

Sukie sipped her ginger beer. She watched the undertaker over the rim of the glass. "Where is he?"

"Roarer? 'E's in the conservatory. Didn't seem right to put 'im in the Chapel o' Rest even if it's not consecrated. Quite a job, it was, makin' the box. 'E's a large lion an' Mr. Tabora 'ad 'im stuffed rampant."

"Will you open it up again before he's buried?"

Mr. Scales shook his head. "Mr. Tabora nailed 'im up with 'is own 'ands. 'E put Roarer's favorite whip between the paws an' saluted 'im like 'e used to in the ring. Pathetic, it was. I've 'ad quite a few circus clients, trapeze, tightrope an' such, but I'm tellin' you ..." He looked round and found that he had been talking to an empty stool.

" 'Angin's too good for 'im," said Doris from the Ladies' Bar. " 'E ought to be made an example of."

"They'll get 'im," said Lil. "Paper says they expeck an arrest hourly."

" 'Eard that one before," said Mae. "Wish 'e'd got my feet. Then 'e'd be sorry."

Sukie was back in the kitchen.

"Mrs. Filby," she said. "I have nobody to whom to turn."

"All right," said Mrs. Filby, resigned. "What is it this time?"

Sukie was a Heap. Lack of opposition unnerved her. "Suppose," she said feebly, "that you had something that you didn't want anybody to know you'd got ..."

This, during the lean war years, had happened to Mrs. Filby several times. "Meat?" she asked briskly.

"Well, yes. Yes. Meat."

"Wrap it up, put your name on it, an' take it to the butcher to put in the fridge. Give 'im a cut to keep 'im 'appy." She registered mild cunning. "You got a ham?" she said.

"No, I haven't."

"Lamb?"

"No."

"One o' those African geese off the Round Pond then."

"Nothing like that."

Mrs. Filby frowned. "You 'aven't gone an' done a pig, 'ave you, dear?"

Sukie had only wanted the loan of Mrs. Filby's toolshed for a couple of hours. She had not intended to tell her for what reason. She was, however, incapable of keeping a secret. Before she could control her tongue, she had said, "It's a man."

Mrs. Filby took the lid off the saucepan and looked at the cod. "Come off it, dear," she said.

"It's true."

"Well, *really*!" said Mrs. Filby.

"He's dead." Sukie shivered. "He was murdered."

"*Murdered*! Now of that," said Mrs. Filby warmly, "I do *not* approve!" She was startled, but not unduly horrified. She had once served in a public house in Limehouse. Years among the regulars there had rendered her insensitive to shock. She flopped the steaming cod into a colander and turned off the gas. "It's against the law," she said severely. "You'll 'ave to ring up the Station an' tell Albert."

"No," said Sukie quickly. "I like Albert, but he'll think it was me. You see," she hesitated, "you mustn't tell a soul, but I am the granddaughter of Hannah Heap."

Everybody in the neighborhood knew this, but Mrs. Filby saw no reason to disillusion her favorite customer. "They got a lovely waxwork

20

of 'er in Madame Tussaud's," she said noncommittally. "Right next to that 'orrible Frog." She slid the cod on to a plate, poured tomato sauce over it, and began to eat. "Albert won't 'old that against you," she added reassuringly.

"He might. Same method. Axe."

Mrs. Filby looked thoughtful. Suddenly appalled, she dropped her fork. "Not your old man?" She choked.

"Oh, *no!*" Sukie patted her on the back. "It's only Mr. Bentley."

Mrs. Filby wiped her eyes and drew a breath of relief. "Serve 'im right!" she said. She saw Sukie's face and added quickly, "You shouldn't 'ave killed 'im. It's not right!"

"I didn't." Sukie began to speak very fast. "A man came on a bicycle. He was small but very strong. He killed Mr. Bentley at once, then got on to his bicycle and rode away. It was one of those petrol bicycles, blue."

Mrs. Filby removed a bone from her mouth. She did not believe this story, but neither was she willing to believe that Sukie had committed murder. "Might 'ave been the Strangler," she mumbled.

Sukie beamed. "I hoped you'd say that."

Mrs. Filby stopped eating and looked up at her sideways. "Why?" she said suspiciously.

Sukie did not answer this. Instead she said. "I've got to get him out of the house. Hugh doesn't like him and we've got no proper place to put him. I wondered if I could bring him here."

Mrs. Filby was not quite satisfied. After all, Hannah too had been small and delicately made. She got up and scraped the bones off her plate into the dustbin. "You *sure* it wasn't you, dear? I couldn't 'elp you, not if you'd done anythin' against the law."

"I haven't. Truly."

Mrs. Filby examined the earnest, freckled face and felt a pang of remorse. "Well," she said without enthusiasm, "you can bring 'im 'ere just for the night. 'E'll 'ave to go down in the cellar, though."

"I thought of the toolshed."

"No. I got cress in there." She pointed her head at Sukie. "Only one night, mind, to give you time to look around."

"Yes. I promise. I've got a plan."

Mrs. Filby took the red mullet out of the oven, filleted it, and offered it to Mossop. The cat cleared his throat and lay down to eat. "You be careful," she said. "I *know* your plans."

Sukie hurried away. She now needed expert criminal assistance. She knew exactly where to find it. She went in search of Beecher.

As usual, he was in the public bar. It was the first time Sukie had been

21

in there. There were no settees and the linoleum on the floor was of an inferior quality. There was a blunt notice about spitting. The local grocer and the butcher's second string were playing darts. They looked at her resentfully. Beecher was propped against the counter swilling the rough cider locally known as Hit Me Once.

Sukie approached him diffidently. He looked tough, strong, brutal. She had never spoken to him before. She waited for a moment for her courage to catch up with her determination.

"Good evening," she said bravely. "I would like to buy you a drink."

Beecher's small, turreted eyes turned slowly. He looked at her with distrust. Nobody ever bought Beecher a drink. Periodically, just to keep his hand in, he would pick a pocket and so indirectly have a drink at an enemy's expense, but nobody, for as long as he could remember, had ever bought him a drink voluntarily. He immediately suspected a trick. He curled his squashed lip. Sukie bought a pint of cider and a ginger beer.

"I am in great trouble," she said, "and I need your help."

Beecher opened his primitive mouth, poured the cider into it, and turned away. Sukie caught his arm.

"There is a murdered man in my house," she murmured.

Beecher jumped. "*Wot?*" he said involuntarily. His face hardened. "Cock," he said coldly.

"Promise," said Sukie.

Beecher stared at her. His face sagged. He thought nothing of larceny, robbery with violence, or even arson, but he drew the line at murder. " 'Oo creased 'im?" he asked, watching Sukie as if she might explode.

Sukie met his eyes. She knew that she was safe with Beecher, that he hated policemen in much the same way that she hated snakes. She also knew that she had got to hold his interest. "I did," she said firmly.

Beecher made a disgusting noise at the back of his throat. "You an' 'oo else?" he jeered.

"I am not strong," said Sukie, "but I am intensely wiry. I hit him with an axe and his head broke like an egg."

"Axe?"

"Axe."

Beecher knew all about Hannah Heap. It occurred to him that one might inherit a talent for murder in the same way as he had inherited a knack with safes. It might as well have been a fortune, an ability, or odd eyes. If it were a taste for homicide, it was just too bad. "I don't like stiffs," he said, stalling for time.

"I didn't mean to kill him. It was just one of those things."

Beecher wiped his nose on the back of his hand and sat down. If she

22

had ironed somebody, he reasoned, it was principally the fault of her forebears. It seemed unfair that she should take the rap. "Wot's in it for me?" he asked after a thoughtful pause.

Twenty minutes later, he jerked his abominable cap over his eyes and sauntered out of the bar. The local grocer watched him uneasily. He did not like the gleam in the man's eye. With a reputation like Beecher's, that gleam usually spelt trouble. The butcher's second string, remembering that there were eleven Hungarian turkeys on his counter, left immediately at a brisk trot. Sukie sat down in a corner and waited.

It was nearly closing time before Beecher returned. He did not speak to Sukie but he glanced in her direction and nodded almost imperceptibly. Sukie rose at once and went without a word.

It was very dark in the mews. She walked fast, her heels tapping on the cobbles. The wind had risen again and was hissing through the weeds on the wasteland. At the end of the road, there was a car without headlights parked in a ruined arch. As she came closer, Sukie recognized George Heap's drophead coupé. Her uncle was sitting behind the wheel with his coat collar turned up. She greeted him with a formula which dated back to her childhood.

"Watcher Heap. You asleep?"

George Heap answered automatically in kind, "Closer creep and have a peep." He sounded impatient. "Have you seen this Bentley fellow? We had an appointment."

Sukie spoke without thinking. "He won't come. He can't." Hastily, she added, "He's gone."

"Gone? Gone where?"

Sukie waved an arm vaguely behind her. "Away," she said.

"Up North?"

"I don't know."

George Heap drummed his fingers on the steering wheel. "Typical," he said bitterly. "Why did he not let me know?" His niece did not answer this and he added grimly, "I suppose he intends to pester you from afar."

"Oh, no. We've heard the last of him." Sukie knew that she must get away before she told him too. "It's all right," she said, backing. "I fixed it."

George Heap wound down his window. "Sukie. Come here."

"No. I'm going home. Good night."

She turned and ran. As she raced into Cork Street, she heard him start up the car. She thought that he would follow her, but as she reached her front door, she heard the car purr away towards Tite Street. She let herself in and went through to the kitchen.

23

Hugh was in there. His hair stood on end. He was bending over the sink scrubbing the bloodstained axe with Vim.

"Where have you been?" he demanded. His voice was that of a man at the end of his tether.

"I went for a walk," said Sukie. "I was knocked down by a horse and cart."

Hugh dropped the murder weapon in the sink. He took two steps towards his wife, raised his arm as if to strike her, then checked himself.

"Sukie," he said in a stifled voice. "Listen, Sukie."

"Yes, darling."

"Look. I love you. I love you dearly – but *you've got to stop lying*. Do you understand?"

"Yes."

"Where have you been?"

"In the local. Where's the body?"

Hugh ran a hand through his hair and looked hunted. "I don't know," he said hoarsely. "Oh, God, this is awful!"

"What is?"

"The bell rang. Then a man burst in with a scarf over his face and held me up. He kept me covered while he stuffed Bentley into a sack and then made off with him over the back wall."

Sukie smiled. "Really, darling!"

"I know, I know. But it's true, I swear it's true."

"He had a clubfoot perhaps?" she asked kindly.

"Don't be idiotic! Well, yes. He had actually. At least the left dragged a little. Sukie, you've got to believe me!"

Sukie raised her eyebrows. She laced her hands together, looked down at them, and sighed tolerantly. She was delighted. Beecher had followed his instructions to the letter.

## CHAPTER 4

GEORGE HEAP returned to his club in a mean mood. He went up to his room thinking of the obnoxious Bentley. In spite of Sukie's denial, he was sure that the man intended blackmail, that even now he was crouching doglike in a northbound train planning the threatening letter. Gnawing his lip, George Heap brushed his hair, put a fresh gardenia into his buttonhole, and started downstairs to dinner.

Passing the bathroom, he heard somebody inside splashing and humming nasally. It was Tribling. He was having another of his debilitating baths. What was more, he was smoking again. George Heap heard the soft hiss of cigar ash on the wet floor.

In the hall, he picked up a late-night paper. He was still in the news. There was another picture of the bomb site, also one of Detective Inspector Stoner bending over a small shrub. George Heap remembered that shrub. It had had thorns. He hoped that the policeman had also had trouble with it.

Passing through into the dining room, he reflected with satisfaction that the Heaps were back in the headlines. Hannah, of course, had been a *cause célèbre*. His grandfather, too, had had his moment in the limelight. He had invented a primitive form of submachine gun. It had quickly become obsolete, but not before it had killed almost everybody in the Sudan. Sir Frank's effigy at Madame Tussaud's was in an honorable position on the first floor. Hannah, who had killed only five, was downstairs in the Chamber of Horrors. In George Heap's opinion, this was intolerably unjust. Equally so was the fact that Sir Frank and Hannah had been judged sane, while Victoria, who had killed nobody at all, had been certified. He had protested strongly to the relevant authorities. They were, however, not in sympathy with his views. From that day, George Heap nursed a deep grudge against formal justice and its administrators.

His anger had partially waned before he found a means of expressing it. Returning home from a long weekend, he was held up by a bandit just outside Maidenhead. He regarded this attention as infernal cheek. By the time he had finished expressing his disapproval, the man was dead. George Heap justified this lapse to himself as an informal protest against the M'Naughten Rules which had hanged his mother. In recent more honest moments, he admitted the experience had been stimulating. A *bon viveur* caught in the maw of postwar austerity, he was intolerably bored. He evolved The Game. The second catastrophe was premeditated.

He was disappointed that this time he had drawn Inspector Stoner as his opponent. The man, he felt, was not worthy of him. He had looked forward to pitting his wits against somebody older, shrewder, more experienced.

He sat down at his usual table and ordered his dinner. He had eaten his sole and was toying with a partridge before Tribling appeared. The little man came half-running down the aisle between the tables. He stopped beside George Heap and gave him a pixie smile. His hair was still damp. He looked greedily at the partridge and contrived, without appearing to move, to joggle the table.

George Heap studied him. Under the tablecloth, his hands twitched. His expression was benign. He smiled at Tribling.

"You're going to regret that," he said.

By the time Hugh and Sukie Chandor had buried the axe-head on the wasteland, burnt the handle in their boiler, and tidied up the scene of the crime, it was after midnight. They ate a late dinner in the kitchen.

"Sukie," said Hugh suddenly, hoping to shock her into an admission, "*Why did you kill him?*"

Sukie smiled. "I saw you coming," she said.

"Are you *never* going to tell me what happened?"

"I already have. You didn't believe me."

"I know perfectly well when you're lying."

This infuriated her. "All right," she snapped. "He was climbing a tree. He climbed right to the top and then jumped out on to his head."

Hugh ground his teeth. He determined not to say another word. Seven minutes later, the desire to practice his cross-examination got the better of him. "Do you *honestly* think," he burst out, "that a story like that would stand up in court?"

"We're not in court."

"Which tree?"

"That tatty old tree on the corner."

"There is no tree on the corner."

"Not that one. The other."

Hugh knew that it was hopeless, that if he persisted he would almost certainly lose his temper but he could not stop. "I see," he said furiously. "And would you mind telling me how you got him back here?"

"Not at all. I brought him back in a rickshaw."

Hugh pushed back his chair and left the room. He tried to slam the door but the handle came off in his hand. He hurled it at the front door and marched upstairs into the drawing room. Half an hour later, when he was beginning to cool down and had settled in a determined manner to some revision on Jurisprudence, Sukie appeared.

She had apparently forgotten her irritation. She kissed the top of his head and said, "Darling, isn't there a thing called Justifiable Homicide?"

Hugh, seething again, brushed her aside. He did not answer.

"All right," she said. "Now I've taken it."

Hugh took no notice.

"Don't you want to know what I've taken?"

"No."

"Umbrage."

"All right. Take it."

"Yes, I have."

"Good."

"Good back," said Sukie angrily. She sniffed defiantly and stalked away to bed.

Hugh sat in his chair and stared into the fire. *Murder!* he thought, appalled all over again. His wife had committed murder! *Unlawfully killing a reasonable creature in being and under the King's peace with malice aforethought express or implied, the death following within a year and a day.* He shuddered. It was difficult to associate Sukie with murder. But then it was almost impossible to associate the photographs he had seen of the frail, delicate Hannah with the hideous atrocity she had perpetrated. His wife was a killer! He tried to comfort himself. Death by violence was not necessarily murder. Could it have been, as Sukie herself had suggested, Justifiable Homicide? *That the prisoner did commit the homicide, but the circumstances were such that no guilt attached to her.* He looked up the examples. The warder who killed a convict in preventing an escape; the officer who slew an unruly Hindu in suppressing a riot; the constable who used fatal force in arresting a felon; the hangman who dispatched as many as would fit into his schedule and got paid for it. No, it was no good. None of these related to Sukie's crime. Justifiable Homicide was out.

What about Excusable? *That the prisoner did commit the homicide, but the circumstances were such as to amount to misadventure.* He looked up Excusable and read about an axe-head which had flown off. That would not do, either. Sukie's axe-head had been firmly wedged on. He had examined it himself. He read about the bungling surgeon, the woman defending her child, the loutish footballer. No, it was not Excusable either.

Hugh sighed. He was just about to consider his old enemy, Manslaughter, when he heard a stealthy footstep on the stairs. He put down his books and sat listening. Silence. He picked up the books again and heard the back door close softly. He leapt up, spilling the books, and charged downstairs. He did not stop to turn on the lights in the hall. He blundered along the passage to the kitchen. A tap was dripping into the sink but otherwise there was not a sound. He snatched open the door and ran into the garden. It was very dark and for a moment he could see nothing. There was sleet in the wind. He shivered and turned up his collar. He stood listening.

"Sukie," he called softly.

No answer. The wind rattled the bare branches of the fig tree. A click. It was a door closing, the back door of the Carp. Hugh scrambled through the rockery and banged his knee on the sundial. He misjudged the distance between the crazy paving and the back wall. The latter caught him across the diaphragm and winded him. He clambered over the wall, marched across the yard, and into the kitchen of the public house.

Mr. Tooley had gone to bed at half past eleven. Although only those who knew him well would have realized it, he was drunk.

He had snitched only eleven drinks that evening, which a year or two ago would have had as little effect on him as a cup of tea, but he had lately reached the stage of being so thoroughly soused in alcohol that two drinks were enough to set him right back where he had left off the previous session.

His last cure had been in September, a mere two months ago. It could not have taken properly because he had begun to see Them again, the hatefully familiar tadpoles, the sly ones, the vague shapes of seagulls. The marmoset was back again too, the white marmoset which sat at the base of his neck, behind his head where he could never quite see it. This time he had first noticed it while pouring a gin for Miss Dogtinder. It had been swinging from an electric fixture. As he drew a pint of cider for Beecher, the phasma leapt on to his shoulder and wound hairy little fingers around his ears. Mr. Tooley knew only one answer to this recurring mirage. He had another drink.

Now he lay in bed unable to sleep and Charleyboy sat on the brass ball at the end of the bed and watched him with its missing eyes. Just after one-thirty he knew that he could bear it no longer. He lurched out of bed and turned on the light. He pulled on his dressing-gown, shook the scorpions out of his slippers, and crept downstairs to steal a drink.

He padded quietly into the kitchen to find Mrs. Filby's electric torch. He caught a quick glimpse of man standing by the refrigerator. Knowing that he was not genuine, Mr. Tooley ignored him. He found the torch in the dresser drawer, turned it on, and made his way cautiously down the steep stone stairs to the cellar.

Here lay the barrels of beer and cider, each with its long rubber feed disappearing through the ceiling to the bar above. Mr. Tooley glanced at their fat, shadowy stomachs and sneered. He was more interested in the well-stocked shelves of spirits. Shuffling across, he played the torch over them. He licked his lips. He saw the man in the sou'wester lying on the floor and decided to have a go at the rum.

He seized the bottle, stepped back, and worried the cork with his teeth. It slid out without a sound. The fumes rose straight into Mr. Tooley's grateful nostrils. He raised the bottle with shaking hands, tilted it, and took a long swallow. He grunted, shook himself, and drank again. The rum rolled down his devastated gullet into a troubled pool of gin, port, and Guinness. As it sank, Mr. Tooley's courage rose; by the time it had consolidated its position the Carp's second-in-command was once again Warrior Tooley Fearless Drummer Boy of the Boxer Rising. He replaced the bottle in its scabbard at his hip and fell into step with the regiment. Then he broke rank and contemptuously kicked the man on the floor.

He hurt his foot.

He dropped the bottle of rum and reeled against the wall. With a low, stricken moan he steadied himself, gave the order to retreat, and ran whimpering upstairs. He rushed into his room, fell trembling into bed, and drew the marmoset into his arms for comfort.

Hugh, still standing quietly in the Carp kitchen, heard the crash of breaking glass in the cellar and shambling footsteps running upstairs. A door slammed somewhere overhead and then there was silence. He was just about to strike a match when he heard somebody coming along the passage. It was somebody in sneakers walking without any pretense of stealth. *I'm trespassing*, he thought. He ducked behind the refrigerator.

"Put up your hands," said Sukie's voice, "or I will shoot you dead with my gun."

Hugh leapt from his hiding place and grabbed her. "What the hell do you think you're doing?" he said.

"Oh," said Sukie without enthusiasm. "It's you."

"I'm going home," said Hugh fiercely. "And you're coming with me."

"No, I'm not. I'm busy."

Hugh took her by the back of the sweater and propelled her towards the door.

"You put me down," she said. "You're outnumbered. I've got an accomplice."

Hugh picked her up bodily. She snatched at the handle of the mangle and held on. The iron legs squeaked across the floor. Hugh braced himself to make another effort. In the moment of silence, he heard somebody coming up the steps from the cellar, somebody walking slowly as if he were tired. Sukie seized her opportunity. She wriggled away from him and dodged behind the kitchen table.

The door opened slowly, scraping along the linoleum. The beam of a torch raced across the floor and picked up Sukie. Then it doubled back and focused on Hugh's foot. Hugh withdrew it. The beam followed it, then flicked upwards straight into his eyes. Blinking, Hugh fumbled for his matches. The first one broke. He tried again. As the small flame rose he saw that on the far side of the torch was the masked man who had held him up before dinner. The scarf over his lower features had slipped. His misshapen nose hung over it like a cactus. It was the man Beecher and he had one arm around the waist of Mr. Bentley. The stiffened body leaned against him as if they were about to dance.

Hugh dropped the match and hurled himself at Beecher. Beecher dropped Mr. Bentley and swayed out of range. Mr. Bentley fell rigidly backwards and hit the floor with a crash. Hugh sprang at Beecher again. He did not see him move, but he found himself sitting on the floor fighting for breath. Beecher picked up Mr. Bentley and made for the back door. Sukie ran around the table and followed him. The door shut behind them with a click.

Hugh rose painfully. He stood for a moment trying to regain his breath, then leapt at the back door. Out in the yard, the wind struck him sideways. It ballooned the legs of his trousers and snatched at his hair. There was no sign of Sukie or Beecher.

He stood for a moment at a loss. On his left was Alistair's back yard and studio, on his right, Mr. Scales' conservatory and stack of seasoned wood. There was a low, unpleasant laugh from the darkness on his left. A small lantern suddenly appeared. Alistair Starke stood up on the far side of the wall and unwrapped himself from the holds of a dirty plaid rug. He was wearing a leather jerkin over his pajamas and smiling broadly.

"Fancy meeting you!" he said.

Hugh looked around quickly. Still no sign of Sukie or Beecher. "And what the hell are *you* doing?" he demanded.

Alistair sniggered. "Looking for my Muse. What about you?"

Hugh thought fast. "Just checking up. I thought I heard a prowler."

"I have been here for some time, *amigo*. There was no prowler. *But* approximately three minutes ago, two – shall we say, poltergeists? – passed this way. They are at present on Mr. Scales's premises. I have, so to speak, been enjoying a seat in the stalls."

Hugh's heart sank. "You can't see a thing," he said. "It's too dark."

Alistair propped himself against the wall. "I saw all right. My eyes are equally good in infrared or ultraviolet."

"I never liked you," said Hugh. He picked up a lump of coal and threw it at the lantern.

"Temper, temper," said Alistair. He laughed. "You'll regret that, chum. I've got you in the palm of my hand."

"You go to hell!" said Hugh. He succumbed to an overwhelming impulse. He laid a hand on Alistair's face and pushed.

"Direct action," said Alistair from behind the wall. "It dates you, comrade. Litigation is the thing these days. Oh, you monster! I'm bleeding."

"Good," said Hugh. *Felonious wounding*, he thought.

He ran across the yard and climbed over the wall into Mr. Scales's parsley bed. The cat Mossop had been lying quite near enjoying the scent of the herb. He sprang up with a buzz of fright and streaked into a pyramid of elm planks. Hugh, startled, lit a match. The wind snuffed it out immediately. Hugh stood still, waiting for Alistair to follow him. He looked up at the back of Mr. Scales's house, thinking briefly that he too probably had a body on his hands; but his would be legal. The house was in complete darkness. There was no sound in the yard behind him. He stretched an exploring hand and found the glass panes of the conservatory. They had a crust of hoar frost. He felt his way along them to the door. He gave it a gentle push and it swung inwards. There was a dim light inside.

The building was not large. It was domed and its glass walls were painted black on the inside. On the larger panes somebody had painted stylized cinerary urns, plumes, and funereal mottoes. Trails of dusty ivy had infiltrated through a hole in the roof and hung in dark festoons. Dead leaves lay in heaps in the corners of the floor. The air was heavy with the smell of leaf mold and formaldehyde.

A torch stood on end on a slab of dirty marble. It was shrouded in a black scarf and gave only a feeble light. In the center of the room were two rough trestles upon which stood an oddly shaped open coffin. Bending over it, with the light on the unfamiliar under-planes of their faces were Sukie and Beecher. Hugh shut the door and lifted the scarf off the torch.

Beecher and Sukie straightened up. Beecher's hand leapt to his pocket. He stepped quickly in front of something lying on the floor. It was Mr. Bentley, pushed against the wall and still wearing his sou'wester.

Hugh shut his eyes. *I must not panic*, he thought. *These things do happen. Every year in the British Isles there are approximately two hundred murders. Only one third of the murderers are ever brought to trial and half that number are acquitted or reprieved. I must not lose my head. I must keep calm.* He opened his eyes.

Beecher, apparently thinking that Hugh was not worth bothering about, was leaning inside the coffin pulling at something. Hugh clenched his hands. He was unable to take his eyes off the man. He half expected him to bring forth another body, perhaps two or even three. He thought wildly of Landru, of Smith, of Hannah Heap. Beecher pushed back his cap and leaned again into the coffin, spreading his arms. He flexed his legs. He stood up slowly, staggering slightly, and lifted out a large, stuffed lion.

For a second Hugh was convinced that it was alive but somehow paralyzed. Its eyes gleamed green and its lip was drawn back in an ugly snarl.

31

Beecher stood it on the floor. It was proudly rampant, the great throat arched, the ears flat against the shaggy head. It was fixed to a platform of dyed grass. Hugh, dazed, put out a hand and touched it. The coarse mane felt strangely warm. Beecher picked up Mr. Bentley, and lowered him into the coffin. Hugh started forward.

"You can't do that!" he said in a horrified whisper. "That's ..."

"Shush!" hissed Sukie. "And anyway," she added, "legally, *what* is it? It isn't anything. Nobody ever thought of it before."

Hugh was distracted again by Beecher. The man had a mouthful of nails and he was doing something spasmodic inside the coffin. He looked up at Sukie.

" 'Ear me 'ammerin' without no noise?" he said quietly. He hammered again. It did not make a sound.

He picked up the lion and tried to get him into the coffin. The head stuck out. Beecher tried him the other way up but the platform would not go in. He picked up an odd-looking saw and sliced Roarer off his base. The saw made no noise at all. Beecher glanced at Sukie.

" 'Ear it?"

She shook her head.

"Didn't think you would. Nobody can 'cept dogs." He tried again to get the lion into the coffin.

*They're mad*, thought Hugh. *Both of them. They'll never get away with this. They'll get about twenty years – if they're not hanged. I could still try to get her off on a manslaughter charge.* "Sukie," he said, "I appeal to you. Come home."

"No," said Sukie. "*You* go home."

Hugh had heard that tone from all three surviving Heaps. He knew that it was hopeless. It was no use trying to carry her off bodily in Beecher's presence. He stood uncertainly wondering what to do next. Neither of them was taking the slightest notice of him. They had given up trying to get the lion into the coffin. Sukie was kneeling on its back and helping to screw on the lid of the casket. Hugh turned suddenly and walked out of the conservatory. He stepped over the parsley bed and felt his way along the wall. He climbed into his own garden and brushed the grit off his hands.

"Sleep tight," said Alistair Starke's disembodied voice. "Personally, I'm staying for the third act."

"Oh, shut up!" said Hugh savagely.

Alistair clicked his tongue. "Tetchy!" he said. "For a prospective officer of the law, I think you're being very, very *naughty*."

Hugh did not answer. He strode across the rockery, chipped his shins

32

on the sundial, and marched into the kitchen. He stamped upstairs and, turning on the lights in his room, walked rapidly up and down hitting things with the flat of his hand.

Miss Dogtinder lived in a Nissen hut in the garden of Marigold Tossit's house. She had chosen this home because it was the nearest available to the bomb site. She regarded this first as an encroachment in the medieval sense, and then as her own particular plantation. It provided her with a supply of vegetables, the more gallant herbs, and also with pasture for her goat.

She was outwardly the most respectable of Mrs. Filby's customers. She had the firm manner of a chatelaine and a slight mustache which subtly enhanced her prestige. A vegetarian, a herbalist, a staunch believer in astrology, she had a habit of lapsing occasionally into outmoded slang. She had for over ten years been making a comfortable income from various herbal remedies and a small but cranky clientele.

Tonight it was nearly two o'clock before Miss Dogtinder decided to settle to her regular eight hours of insomnia. She was just about to extinguish her pressure lamp when her supersensitive ears told her that there was somebody moving stealthily around in the next-door garden.

She stumped over to the window and peered through the curtains. Due perhaps to daily infusions of hawkweed and loosestrife, she could see almost equally well in light or darkness. She saw the horrid sight at once.

Just above the wall, fitfully visible between the bushes, was the head of a large animal. It was moving jerkily towards the Chandors' back door. It was, incredibly, a lion.

Miss Dogtinder was no coward. Her lips tightened. She raised her chin, flung open her corrugated door, and charged across the garden to Marigold's house as fast as her webbed feet would carry her. Breathing hard, she clambered in through the larder window and made for the telephone. She snatched off the receiver and briskly dialed 999.

## CHAPTER 5

Mr. Tooley woke up at 8:04. This was two hours earlier than usual, but last night's session had impaired his focusing and forced him to use guesswork when setting the alarm. He opened his gritty eyelids slowly, lying quietly, smoothing the sheet with his feet; he looked around under his eyelashes for the marmoset. There was no sign of it.

Easing himself out of bed, he tiptoed to the cupboard, picked up a heavy bookend, and jerked open the door. Except for his other pair of shoes, the cupboard was empty. Mr. Tooley's tiny eyes ranged around the room. There were only two other places where his chimera might be hiding. One was the wastepaper basket, the other was under the cushion on the armchair. Mr. Tooley picked up a carafe of water and poured it into the wastepaper basket. There was no movement from within.

Mr. Tooley sucked in his cheeks. He glanced once at the cushion on the armchair and began to fumble into his clothes. He knew that bending over to tie up his shoes would make him giddy, so he did not attempt it. Cramming four aspirins into his mouth, he picked up a walking stick and prepared to go in search of coffee. As he passed the armchair, he gave the cushion a terrible blow with the stick. Then he nipped out of the room, locked the door, grunted, and went downstairs smiling.

In the kitchen, Mrs. Filby was eating bread and marmalade. Mossop was crouching over a saucer sniffing at a mess of soft-boiled eggs. On the table by the place laid for Mr. Tooley lay the remains of the Moussec glass he had broken the previous morning. Mr. Tooley knew the technique. Mrs. Filby would put the pieces there every morning until he had replaced them with a new glass. He sat down and poured himself a cup of coffee without lifting the percolator off the table. He lowered his head and drank from the cup where it stood. Even though his hands did not touch the cup, his face was trembling so much that the teaspoon rattled in the saucer. Mr. Tooley clamped his thumb on to it and held it down.

Mrs. Filby ignored him. Both knew exactly what the other was thinking. Mrs. Filby was wondering whether to crush his last flicker of resistance by laying before him a plate of fried eggs in a pool of grease. She knew that he was expecting it and was even now steeling himself against it. Mr. Tooley knew all this. He did not look at her. He sat patiently awaiting the result of her decision. Even the thought of eggs made him cringe. He drank some coffee and wrote the word Monkey on the tablecloth with the handle of his teaspoon. The moment passed. Mrs. Filby decided against eggs. Mr. Tooley gave her a glance of dumb gratitude. He grunted and cleared his throat with a rattle.

"Dead man in the cellar," he remarked.

"Eh?" said Mrs. Filby testily. "Speak up."

"Man dead in the cellar."

Mrs. Filby put down her knife. She knew that the body had been removed. She had checked up. "Now don't you start *that* again," she said with a show of anger.

34

Mr. Tooley wriggled uneasily. He had a moment of doubt. " 'Strue," he said uncertainly. "Sou'wester."

"Fed up with you talkin' wild," said Mrs. Filby. "Dead man in the cellar indeed!"

Mr. Tooley turned over his spoon and gave it a little push. "There was," he said obstinately.

Mrs. Filby hit the table with the crumb brush. " 'Old your tongue!" she snapped.

Mr. Tooley was silent. He was staring at the butter. He noticed for the first time that it was imprinted all over with the footmarks of some small animal with diminutive and unopposable thumbs.

"It's only the police," said Sukie, leaning further out of the bedroom window.

Hugh sat up and yawned. The bell rang again. He remembered the events of the night before and sprang out of bed. He seized his wife by the back of her skirt and jerked her off the window ledge.

"Give me time to think," he said, frantically rubbing his eyes. "They may not have a warrant. We must get a lawyer. The best. I'll ring up ..."

"Really, darling!" said Sukie. "It's only Albert. He probably wants a cuppa."

Hugh let her go and sat down on the edge of the bed. He breathed out slowly through his nose, shook his head, and tried to think. When he looked up, Sukie had gone. He heard her running downstairs two at a time. Then the front door opened and Albert's boots tramped heavily across the hall. Hugh got up, went out on to the landing, and leaned over the banisters. Albert's broad, navy blue back was just disappearing into the kitchen. Sukie followed him. She was carrying the morning paper. Hugh saw the word Strangler in two-inch type.

"Pss-st!" he hissed.

Sukie looked up over her shoulder. She giggled "Pss-st, back," she said.

"Come here."

"Albert saw that lion I told you about," she said. "Isn't it exciting?"

"*Come here!*"

Sukie went into the kitchen and closed the door.

Hugh straightened up slowly. He walked quietly across the landing and pushed open the bathroom door. He prayed without hope that Roarer had gone, had never been there at all, that he had imagined or dreamed the lunatic business of last evening. But the stuffed lion was still there, standing, for want of a better place, in the bath. In the morning light he looked larger, fiercer, more ominous. Hugh swore. He removed the key, locked the door on the outside, and dropped the key into his pajama pocket.

*Larceny*, he thought. *That lion is not mine. I am an accessory to a larceny, recognizing the intent at the time of taking to deprive the owner permanently thereof. I don't even want the damned thing. I hate it.*

He went back into the bedroom and sat down on the bed. Ten minutes later, he heard somebody coming upstairs. He froze, listening. It was either Sukie or Albert. If it were Sukie, she would be in tears and handcuffs; if it were Albert, he had come to confess that, purely as a formality, he was taking Sukie down to the Station for further questioning.

It was Sukie. She was eating an apple and carrying a cup of tea. Hugh leapt to his feet, furious with relief. Sukie offered him the tea, but he only brushed it aside.

"No!" he roared. "How do I know it's not poisoned?" Having gone so far, he had to justify himself. "You've already bumped off one man for no good reason. How do I know who you're going to pick on next?"

"All right," said Sukie amiably. "Make your own tea. Cook your own food, too, if that's the way you feel."

"I intend to."

Sukie sat down and drank the cup of tea.

Hugh, conscious that he was being unreasonable, went over to the window and stared into the back garden. It was a gray morning. The sky was heavy with rain. Marigold Tossit was optimistically hanging up a pink vest to dry in the next-door yard. Hugh leaned against the chest-of-drawers and put on his left sock.

"What did Albert want?" he asked.

"To bring me some chocolate biscuits and ask about the wild lion."

Hugh put his foot back on to the floor with the sock half on. "What wild lion?"

"The one Miss Dogtinder saw rushing around last night. Albert was very worried about me. They were going to patrol the neighborhood."

"Oh, God!"

"Yes. They would probably have sent for nets and stuff if I hadn't thought of something just in time."

"Now listen, Sukie ..."

"Listen yourself." She threw her apple core into the grate. "I said I'd seen the lion. I said I'd opened the door and shushed it into the road."

"You're crazy. You can't shush lions."

"You can if they're full. They get placid. I chased it into the road and followed it in this Austin 10."

"What Austin 10?"

"The one I found abandoned in Tite Street. Black, I said it was."

Hugh walked back to the window. He leaned his forehead against the cold glass. *This is Victoria's fault*, he thought. *People make jokes about mothers-in-law.* "May I ask," he said, "what I was doing all this time?"

"You were asleep. It was rather fun actually. Albert was tremendously bucked. He wrote it all down and had me sign it just as if it was true."

Hugh tore off his sock and hurled it on to the floor. He walked round in a small circle holding on to his hair.

"And then," said Sukie, "the lion turned at bay just by Battersea Bridge. And I drove this Austin 10 straight at it ..."

"I know, I know. It jumped into the river."

"Yes. And I got out to see and it was swimming madly towards the park."

Hugh stared fascinated at his wife. "Do you honestly imagine that Albert believed you?"

Sukie was doing up a suspender. She did not answer. Hugh picked up a shoe and began to beat the heel in his hand.

"How do you know that lions can swim?"

"This one could. I last saw it climbing up the opposite bank and making off into the bushes." She shivered. She saw the scene vividly. "I expect it was after the deer."

Hugh looked at her. "There is no lion, Sukie."

His wife sighed. She went over to the dressing table and began to comb her hair. "Nor there is," she said. She smiled disarmingly.

"Sukie," said Hugh in a half-whisper.

"Mmm?"

"Will you do something for me?"

"I expect so. What?"

Hugh drew a deep breath. "*Will you*," he shouted, "*kindly take your bloody lion out of the bathroom?*"

Sukie dropped the comb. "Why?" she asked, subdued.

Hugh shut his eyes and swallowed. "I want a bath," he said in a controlled voice.

Opposite, Alistair Starke was kneeling at his bedroom window with a pair of field glasses trained on the Chandors' house. Once he saw Hugh come briefly to the window, but after a further twenty minutes without incident he lost interest, stood up, and stretched. Disappointed and biting his fingernails, he padded downstairs into his dirty kitchen. He lit the gas under a saucepan of coffee dregs, tore the heel off a loaf, and anointed it with dripping. Slopping the coffee into a cracked beaker, he carried his meal through the icy wind in the yard to his studio. Trying hard to concentrate, he set to work on a *gouache* after Rouault of a two-faced woman in a hammock. He painted carelessly, making little runs at the canvas, darting back to take another snap at his food. Catching himself for the second time swilling his brush in the coffee, he gave up. He wiped the brush on his pajama jacket and admitted that he was Not In The Mood. He went fretfully back to his house, slouched upstairs, and composed himself in comfort to spy on the Chandors indefinitely.

Above his funeral premises, Mr. Scales snored quietly. He had recently been testing a sample of the new angelskin shrouds. He found these so downy and relaxing that he did not wake until nine o'clock.

Miss Dogtinder, haggard after yet another sleepless night, peered cautiously around her corrugated door, satisfied herself that there was no cover behind which a lion might still be lurking, and sallied forth to see whether her goat had survived.

Beecher and the Boys had breakfast in Lupus Street. They drank black tea and ate toast topped with slices of Hungarian turkey. The faulty gas fire spluttered. A cigar butt, carelessly stamped upon, lay smoldering on the carpet. A pall of smoke hung near the ceiling. A wasp beat its wings on the window pane, desperate to get out into the gray streets, to breathe again.

Beecher stood up suddenly. His chair fell over. He pushed back his cap and dropped one hand into his pocket. The others stopped eating. Without moving their heads they looked at him nervously. He was subject to fits of sudden and terrible violence.

Beecher took his hand out of his pocket, reached across the table, and wrenched the parson's nose off the turkey.

He sat down, satisfied. Periodically he had to horrify them, he had to make certain that he still gave the orders.

Miles Tate-Grahame was eating porridge and kippers. As usual, he had cooked his breakfast on the Bunsen burner in his laboratory. Long ago, he had perfected a method of boning and eating kippers with one hand; with the other, he was oiling a small scale model of a jet air liner. It was a revolutionary design, beautiful, streamlined, a potential dollar earner. But, as always with Miles' inventions, something, somewhere, was profoundly wrong. The difficulty with aero-jets is to devise a light but exceedingly powerful self-starting mechanism. The Tate-Grahame model took off with a bang upon the firing of a charge equivalent in force to that of a .22 rifle.

The Air Ministry, to whom it had been offered, had complimented Miles upon his ingenuity and enclosed the copy of a note from Woolwich Arsenal. This stated that the caliber of the charge to scale would be slightly less than that of a sixteen-inch naval gun. They calculated that this would blow the engine out of the fuselage and destroy the aircraft on the ground. Nevertheless, Miles had not given up hope. He loved his brainchild and refused to scrap it.

When her mother had suddenly eloped with an elderly G.I., Marigold Tossit had been left in charge of the house next door to the Chandors. After a halcyon six months during which she sold everything of any value in order to buy herself an entire new wardrobe, she found herself penniless. To Marigold this was no problem. She adopted a Protector, a kindly old fellow from the North, who visited her every Thursday. They ate chestnuts and toasted crumpets. Occasionally he threw jam at her, but there was, Marigold insisted, nothing Nasty.

She also let her two spare rooms to quiet business gentlemen. The rowdier of these at the moment was the Great Tabora. He had brought with him a red-lined cloak, a signed photograph of Cecil B. de Mille, and the glamour of the circus. In spite of the preliminary brush about Roarer, she was fascinated by the lion tamer. She also felt that if once she could impress him with her unusual and dynamic personality, he might be instrumental in sending her to Hollywood. She believed that the first thing a man laid eyes on in the morning was the object of his thoughts all day. She therefore made a habit of taking Tabora an early-morning cup of tea.

This morning, the day of Roarer's funeral, she bent over him and shook him gently. His tawny eyes flicked open immediately. His foot found the hot-water bottle. He always associated these, when cold, with seals, which he despised and feared. He shuddered. Marigold misunderstood his reaction. She pinched herself surreptitiously in the nose and her large eyes filled with tears.

"We all gotter go," she said softly. "Beggar or king o' the realm. No favors up There."

Both glanced upwards out of the window. There was a heavy black cloud sailing over Battersea Power Station.

"Bet it's got a silver linin'," murmured Marigold. She gave the cloud a mercenary stare.

"Beat it, dumbbell," said Tabora brutally. He kicked impatiently at the sheet. "Go on! Scram!"

Marigold gave him her Young Nun smile and backed out of the room.

The Great Tabora stepped out of bed and into his ringmaster's boots.

He picked up one of the twelve-foot whips he had used in his act and cracked it savagely. He watched with satisfaction as a cloud of plaster fell from the ceiling.

George Heap woke still tormented by the thought of the insufferable Bentley. He was determined to kill him; he was anticipating the deed with an eagerness which none of his previous projects had inspired. Lathering his face before the mirror, he decided that Bentley must be recalled. He would send him a telegram. The phrase *You will hear something to your advantage* occurred to him. It would intrigue the little skinflint, but would it fetch him immediately? George Heap wanted to strangle him as soon as possible.

Perhaps it would be better to summon him professionally, expense no object. That, too, would put a sparkle into the twitching eye. But would it persuade the man to take the express, which left at an ungodly hour, or would he dawdle down by the slow train? What about *Return. Prepared to talk turkey.* George Heap grinned wolfishly. He began to laugh. He roared with laughter. The razor slipped and he cut himself. He turned faint at the sight of his own blood.

Mrs. Pickett, the charwoman, was known in the Ladies' Bar as Doris. Late as usual, she arrived at the Chandors' house at ten o'clock, an hour after Hugh had left for the Inner Temple. She greeted Sukie with the news that she had been nationalized. She was now a member of the House Workers' Union. Her services could be commanded by anybody who got in touch with the H.W.U., which she pronounced Who.

"We was going to be initiated by Stewart Granger," she said with pride, "but 'e couldn't come. Lil says they didn't know which to do first, us or steel. I s'pose they know what they're up to. They got me guessing, I tell you straight. Mind, that 'ospital scheme was lovely. Got three pair corsets, truss, 'lastic stockin's, pair o' specs, an' I wouldn't like to say what pills an' such." She paused for breath. "Reporter took a pixture o' me yesterday," she added complacently. "Be in the evenin' papers. Gotter union now. 'Spect we'll strike soon, Go Slow or somethink. We ..."

Sukie stopped listening. A few minutes later she made her escape, went upstairs and heaved Roarer off the landing into her bedroom. She put him down by the fireplace, stood back, and studied him. He made the room look much smaller. She pushed him behind an armchair, but his tail showed. She tried to get him under the bed sideways but he would not go. His tail refused either to roll up or even to bend. It was inflexible. Sukie was sitting on his back, nibbling her thumbnail and trying to think of a better place to put him, when Mrs. Pickett appeared.

"Naou!" she said loudly.

"He's not real," said Sukie quickly. To prove this she put her hand into the lion's mouth and smiled reassuringly.

"That's that Roarer," said the charwoman. She made a guillotine gesture with one hand. "I don't like 'im."

"He grows on you," said Sukie earnestly.

" 'E won't on me," said Mrs. Pickett with gathering force. " 'E won't 'ave a chance. I said it to Miss Tossit an' I say it to you. I won't work where 'e is an' that's flat. Dirty brute! 'E brings moths an' 'e *pongs*. It's 'im or me. One of us 'as got to go, an' it's not me or I'll complain to the Who!" She went out and slammed the door.

Sukie considered this ultimatum. Mrs. Pickett could be replaced; but Hugh did not like Roarer either. Sukie felt that eventually the lion might come between them. Sighing, she put on coat and beret and set out for the Carp.

The pub was not yet open. Mrs. Filby was behind the bar secreting a consignment of cigarettes under the counter. She stood up and tugged at her corsets.

Sukie came to the point at once. "Could I borrow the cellar again?" she asked.

Mrs. Filby regarded her narrowly. "What for?"

"I won't say. It's a secret. It's a lion."

Mrs. Filby jerked angrily at one of the brass handles beside her. A jet of bitter splashed into the sink. "Don't you talk to me 'bout lions," she snapped. "Police 'ere first thing askin' 'bout one, Mr. Tabora carryin' on 'bout another, an' now you got one! Suddenly lions all over."

"Mine's stuffed," said Sukie quickly before her tongue ran away with her. "Uncle George shot it in the sterling area." She opened her eyes wide at Mrs. Filby. "*Please*. I'll pay rent for him."

Mrs. Filby stared at her. Sukie reminded her of her own daughter Eudora who had walked out of the house two years ago and never came back. "Why don't you bring me a proper lodger?" she said sullenly. "Everythink you ever brings in is dead." She turned her back and began to splash about in the sink.

Sukie went home through the back garden. She found Mrs. Pickett in the kitchen drinking tea.

"By the way," she said airily, "I'd rather you didn't mention my lion to anybody. It was given to me by a dangerous criminal, and he said ..."

Mrs. Pickett bared her yellow teeth. "Up your jumper!" she said scornfully. "That's Mr. Tabora's lion an' you've stole it."

Sukie cleared her throat. She had been instructed by her uncle that everybody had their price, but she was uncertain about the preliminaries. "Do you think," she began tentatively, "that you could just sort of pretend that you'd never seen him?"

"Naou," said Mrs. Pickett firmly. "I won't never forget it. Gave me a norful turn."

"I see." Sukie drew a circle on the floor with her foot. "You don't think that there are *any* circumstances you could forget it under?"

Mrs. Pickett realized that her employer needed help. "You tryin' to bribe me?" she asked noncommittally.

Sukie blushed. "Well, yes, I am actually."

"Orright," said Mrs. Pickett. "Wot you offerin'?"

"Well, I don't know really. How much is it?"

The charwoman concealed a smile. "Two quid."

Sukie looked relieved. "One," she said, rallying.

"Firty bob. Paid weekly."

"Weekly! But that's ..."

"Now don't you say no nasty words," said Mrs. Pickett sternly, "or I may 'ave one o' me Goes." She drew herself up to her full height and left the room.

Sukie sat down and poured herself a cup of tea. *This case*, she reflected, *is turning out to be a bit more than I bargained for, I mean than for which I bargained*. Her reading and her upbringing had led her to believe that murder was very wicked, sometimes unavoidable, always comparatively simple. One cooked up a motive, chose a prey, dispatched the latter, and humped off. That was all very well in the old days, but currently, with the expansion of the laboratories at Scotland Yard, it had become the vogue to dispose of one's dead in increasingly elaborate manners. Murder had moved with the times and, like everything else, had become more complicated and tedious.

Pouring the untouched cup of tea into the sink, she wished, as had all the Heaps at one time or another, that she could trust her memory about what had actually happened the previous evening. *I don't believe for one moment that I killed him*, she thought. And then, for the hundredth time, *But if I didn't, somebody else did. I must appoint myself Investigator. I must catch this malefactor, this pig. And if at any time it looks as if I am going to catch myself, I can always accept my resignation.*

# CHAPTER 6

SENATOR hated funerals. When he had been eating ferns, he swelled and the shafts of the hearse chafed him. He resented his rubber shoes and the plumes maddened him. He disliked the slow, regulation trot and the pollen from the wreaths made him sneeze.

He was a misfit, never really happy. His dam had died in foaling and, until he was three years old, he had never seen another horse. He therefore believed that he was a man.

Even now, at six, he was uncertain about himself. He knew what the back half of him looked like, but he had nagging doubts about the front. He had grown up entirely dependent upon Mr. Scales. He had been taught to keep his eyes lowered and to rely completely upon his master's touch on the reins. He was always heavily blinkered.

Just after Senator's third birthday, his owner bought a secondhand phantom. Mr. Scales was so excited that he forgot the blinkers. Unadorned, the horse was led on to the bomb site. For the first time outside his stable, he raised his eyes. He was amazed and unnerved by the breadth and sweep of the new horizon.

Then he saw Miss Dogtinder's goat. It stood quite near to him, looking at him curiously. Its horns, its yellow eyes, its uncanny bouquet, kindled some deep atavistic fear in Senator. He was terrified. He leapt two walls and galloped into his stable. He stood there, his head lowered, cheated, disillusioned, betrayed. In those anguished moments he knew that he was not a human being.

For over six weeks he was on the fringe of a nervous breakdown. Then, as he became accustomed to being an animal, his regard for Mr. Scales, the father figure, diminished. He transferred his affections to the goat. But his Ego had taken a beating from which it was never entirely to recover.

Today, he stood shivering and shuffling his hoofs in a strange cemetery. He knew most of the London graveyards, but he had never before been in this one. Listlessly, he looked around him. He noticed that whereas some of the graves were minute, others were abnormally large. Beneath the familiar smell of the flowers, the marble and granite, the wet earth, he detected the faint but unmistakable scent of fur. It was an animal cemetery. That was unusual. So was the fact that his master, with his top hat on the back of his head, was digging.

He could not know that there had been a strike among the gravediggers over a python's funeral. The owner had refused to have it buried coiled up, as was customary, but wanted it stretched out. The gravediggers had taken one look at it and downed shovels immediately. The Great Tabora, Mr. Scales, Alistair Starke, and a representative from one of the popular illustrated weeklies had been obliged to dig Roarer's last resting place themselves. Marigold Tossit stood by in a large black hat with a white wing on the front of it. She was giving a rather sloppy performance because she could remember no film in which there had been an episode of this type.

Grunting, cursing their blistered hands, the men lowered the coffin into the ground. Alistair concealed a grin. He wondered what Sukie would do with Roarer. Tabora unrolled a square yard of turf and spread it over the mound of earth. Then he retrieved his scarlet jacket from the stone effigy of a racehorse, put in on, and did up the brass buttons. He adjusted the epaulettes and put on his top hat. He picked up his whip and cracked it twice in the air.

"Olé!" he shouted.

"Hold it!" said the reporter. He took three pictures. When he had finished, he said "Oak", and departed at a run, furling up his camera.

Tabora's shoulders slumped. He pulled his hat over his eyes and turned away. The others followed silently. Alistair brought up the rear, sucking his blisters and looking thoughtful.

In the Carp, although it was only just afternoon, it was so dark that Mrs. Filby had grudgingly turned on the electric lights. She had installed bulbs of the lowest possible wattage and arranged them in such a way that it was not quite possible for the average-sighted man to be distracted by his newspaper. She noted with annoyance that the gloom was not bothering Beecher.

He was propped against the bar in the Public, destroying a packet of potato crisps and drawing a small diagram on the back of an envelope. His tongue protruded, curling up towards his nostrils, as he added another line to the paper. The diagram was neatly drawn. It showed the facade and environs of a large block of flats.

The drawing finished, Beecher took a stump of red crayon from his pocket, licked it, and laboriously drew a line along a back street and into the side door of the building next door to the flats. The line reappeared on the roof, turned into dots as it leapt the chasm between the two buildings, became solid again as it descended two floors down a drainpipe, and disappeared into a fourth-floor window. Beecher stood back and looked at it with satisfaction. As an afterthought, he fumbled for another crayon and gave the fourth-floor window green curtains. Green was his favorite color.

Albert Chivvers, the local constable, tramped across the bar and looked over his enemy's shoulder. Beecher obligingly stood aside and they admired the diagram together.

"Where's that?" asked Albert.

Beecher leered.

"When?" said Albert.

" 'Aven't made up me mind," said Beecher. "I'll give you a ring."

The empty hearse passed the Carp just before one o'clock. Marigold and Tabora returned to the house in Cork Street, Tabora to change his scarlet jacket for something more conservative, Marigold to change her pink lipstick for something more striking. Mr. Scales led Senator into his stable, unharnessed him, and escorted him back to the bomb site. Both parties, having performed these small rites, headed for the public house.

Alistair Starke went home, combed his beard, and then set out hotfoot to the Chandors' house. He found Sukie in the kitchen ruling lines in a small black notebook.

"Thirsty?" he asked.

"No," said Sukie without looking up.

"The funeral," said Alistair, "was disappointing. The cortège was dominated by a man on a bicycle. In my opinion, bicycles lack dignity, charm, or pictorial promise."

"What do you want?"

Alistair looked out of the window. Miss Dogtinder was leaning over the wall gazing at something in the Chandors' rockery. "I confess," he murmured, "that I was driven here by vulgar curiosity. I ache to know what you have done with Roarer."

Sukie dropped her pencil. She took a long time about picking it up.

Alistair studied the back of her bent head. He decided to take a chance. "Of course," he said chattily, "it seems to me to be a trifle eccentric to bury a veterinary surgeon in a pets' cemetery, but," he spread his dirty hands and smiled, "perhaps I'm old-fashioned."

Sukie stared at him. He stared back with hard eyes. Sukie sighed and pulled her notebook towards her.

"How much?" she asked.

Alistair examined his nails. "Shall we say – five hundred?"

"Don't be silly. I haven't got it."

"Everybody can raise five hundred."

"I can't and nor can you."

Alistair hesitated. "You could, if you prefer it, pay me five pounds a week for two years, three months, and two weeks."

"No, I couldn't. I can't afford it."

"All right. Two pounds a year for ..."

"Yes, I'll do that."

"I meant week. For four years, nine months, and two weeks."

"No, I don't want to."

Alistair tugged at his beard. He did not want to lose his temper. "I won't take a penny less than thirty shillings. That will take six years, five months and ..."

"Oh, shut up!" said Sukie crossly. She made an entry in her notebook. "I'll pay you Saturday like the others."

It was after 1:30 when Hugh came home for lunch. He was still angry. He marched into the kitchen and dumped a string bag on the table. Out of it he took a can of corned beef and a swede the size of a football. He put the swede into the oven, turned on the gas, and marched back the way he had come. Sukie was leaning against the dining-room door watching him, but he took no notice of her. He went out of the house and slammed the door. His wife, who had no pride, followed him. Hugh waited for her on the corner.

"I suggest that you stay at home with your lion," he said coldly. Sukie was annoyed. "You may suggest things until you're blue in the face."

"I'd rather be alone. If you don't mind."

"I do mind."

"I'm afraid I don't mind whether you mind or not."

"Mutual."

Hugh turned the corner and walked a few steps down Wharf Mews. Sukie walked along beside him. He stopped.

"Oh, shut up!" said Sukie.

"You're the one who ought to be shut up."

"Very funny, very funny indeed. Quick on the draw, too."

Hugh hit a tree trunk with the palm of his hand. He closed his eyes. "Go home," he said.

Sukie stamped with both feet at once. "I will not," she shouted.

Miles Tate-Grahame loomed up behind them. "Family squabble?" he inquired pleasantly.

"Mind your own bloody business!" roared Hugh. He stalked away in the direction of the Carp. Sukie whistled a shrill comment after him.

Miles stood on the pavement, gray, lopsided, puzzled.

"Would you say offhand that I was a good wife?" asked Sukie.

The inventor, who was unused to her rapid changes of mood, was taken aback. He peered at her and smiled uncertainly. He had huge teeth. "There was somebody in your garden last night," he said, embarrassed, hoping to steer the conversation into safer channels. He took an involuntary step backwards as Sukie spun around upon him.

"Oh, so there was, was there?" she said. "And what do *you* want?"

Miles decided that she had been drinking and must be humored. "Well, now let me see," he said carefully. He thought hard. Outside his laboratory he had little imagination. "I want some new socks," he said feebly.

Sukie made an entry in her notebook and walked away without another word. Miles, frowning after her, wondered for the first time whether there was any truth in the rumor that her mother was in a mental home.

"...an' *then*," said Marigold Tossit, "Bette Davis comes in. Lovely frock she's got on, off-the-shoulders, cocktail really. An' there 'e *is*, dressing gown, paisley design, corded revers. An' she doesn't know it's 'im, she thinks in 'er ignorance that 'e's 'er brother, an' what's more, she *doesn't even know 'e's blind.* An' ..." She glanced resentfully at Hugh. "You're not listenin'."

"I'm thinking," said Hugh. "I've got a lot on my mind."

"Oh, do talk to me!" said Marigold. She moved a little closer to him on the settee.

Sukie, who was watching from the opposite bar, moved her stool so that she could see better.

"Not often we 'ave the chance," said Marigold. "You're always with Her. D'you think she's as pretty as me?"

"Just at the moment, I don't want to discuss her."

"She doesn't understand you, that's what. Skinny, too, isn't she? Not like me. I'm feminine."

Hugh was not listening.

"D'you like me?" asked Marigold, switching to shock tactics.

"What?"

"D'you want to 'old my 'and?"

"No, thank you."

Marigold took his hand and pressed it against her plump thigh. "Cold 'ands, warm 'eart," she said. She poked him in the ribs. "Bet you're ticklish."

Hugh released his hand, pushed Marigold to her feet, and slapped her bottom. "Go away," he said.

"*You!*" said Marigold, delighted. "I'll *do* you!"

Mrs. Filby, who had missed none of this byplay, sniffed. "See that?" she asked Sukie. " 'Ussy! I'd do '*er*, if I was you."

Mr. Tooley lurched over. "What is life without a wife?" he asked of nobody in particular.

Mrs. Filby saw the look on Sukie's face. Her favorite customer was gazing at Marigold with the sweet, preoccupied calm of Hannah Heap's waxen image in the Chamber of Horrors. She leaned over the counter and seized Sukie by the arm. "Now I didn't mean anythink, dear," she said hastily. "You just forget what I said. I wasn't thinkin'."

Sukie turned. Slowly, her eyes focused on Mrs. Filby's face. Clearly, she had not heard.

Mrs. Filby shook her arm. "Any more larks from you," she said roughly, "an' I'll bar you, see?"

"I'm lookin' forward to the spring nights," said Mae from the Ladies' Bar. "Feel as if you're really livin' then."

"Pekeneses don't '*ave* no brains," said Lil. "They think wiv the back o' their eyes."

"Pass me glass, dear," said Doris. "*Silver play*, I should say."

Mr. Tooley looked at her Moussec regretfully. He was almost sober. Somehow, he had managed to keep his hands off most of the customers' drinks for the entire morning. Those he had appropriated he had not drunk in the proper sense of the word but had secreted in his esophageal pouch. This unusual feature was a closely guarded secret. In the old days, when he was an aggressive young bombardier, he had won many a bet with its assistance. He could, if challenged, drink a pint bottle of whisky straight down. Nobody ever found out that by a slight sideways inclination of the head he could canalize the spirit into the pouch and later, sober as a judge, regurgitate it.

Recently, with spirits at an exorbitant price, the pouch had fallen into disuse. That morning, however, it held three gins, a cherry brandy, and an Advocaat. It had been bypassed only by half a pint of the best bitter. Consequently, Mr. Tooley felt terrible. The marmoset was furious. It was stamping up and down on his shoulder and hitting the top of his aching head with small clenched fists. At each blow Mr. Tooley screwed up his eyes and made a grab at the back of his neck.

This had been going on for some time before Mrs. Filby caught him at it. She marched over and pinched his arm.

"Get outside," she said in a furious whisper. "You're makin' an exhibition o' yourself."

Mr. Tooley shuffled away. He sat in disgrace in the kitchen for thirteen frantic minutes before he knew that one way or another he had to find out whether he was going mad. He found Mrs. Filby's torch, made certain that he was unobserved, and crept down the cellar stairs.

He played the torch over every inch of the dank floor before he turned away, trembling. The broken rum bottle still lay where he had dropped it. But there was no sign of a dead man in a sou'wester, nor any evidence to show that he had ever been there.

Mr. Tooley dragged himself upstairs, went into his bedroom, and locked the door. He leaned out of the window, found the piece of string which led to his cache in the gutter below, and hauled in a bottle of brandy. Sitting down, he drank deeply, then pulled a piece of paper towards him. Writing uncomfortably on his shaking knees, he drafted a letter to the Principal of his favorite Home. *Dear Sir*, he wrote. *I want my money refunded back. Your last cure was not right* ... He had drunk all the brandy before he finished this document. He was about to liberate the bottle strapped under Mrs. Filby's bed when he remembered the alchemy in his secret crucible.

## CHAPTER 7

THERE was a high wall around the Home, with broken glass on top of it. The rain had stopped and the lawns were wet and lush.

Sukie went through the big doors and along the drafty passage. She met the woman in white by the notice board.

The woman tweaked at her cap. "Only ten minutes, mind," she said. She pushed open a baize door and stood aside to let Sukie pass.

Victoria Heap had seen them coming but pretended otherwise. She waited until the woman had rustled away and then frowned.

"I dislike that girl," she said. "I shall speak to the manager. Unless he removes her, I shall go back to the Grand."

No Heap had ever admitted that anyone of their family, with the exception of Sir Frank, was in any way abnormal. Sukie had great faith in her mother's simple wisdom. "Mummy," she said. "I want help and advice."

"Have you been to see Granny lately, darling?"

"Uncle George went. There's a new person next to her. Mummy ..."

"How many did he get?"

"Twenty-eight. He hired an airplane and bombed a bus. Mummy ..."

"Imagine!" said Victoria. "Murder is becoming very spectacular and expensive these days. I believe that even arsenic is subject to purchase tax."

"Yes. Mummy, there's something ..."

"Sukie," said Victoria sternly. "You are concealing something from me. What is it?"

Sukie saw the trap and avoided it. "I won't say."

Victoria wound up her watch. "You must not be secretive, child. It is a deplorable trait."

Sukie studied her. She knew that a moment's mistiming now would mean failure. "I will never tell, never," she said.

"Disobedience in the old shows character. Below the age of fifty it is intolerable. Talking about your uncle George ..."

"We were talking about me concealing something."

"Were we, darling? Are you?"

"Yes. Yes. I am." Sukie looked over her shoulder. "Mummy," she said desperately, "Mr. Bentley is dead."

"Oh?" said Victoria politely. "He was so good with cattle."

"He was murdered."

"Really?"

"In our garden. Hugh is very angry with me."

"Murdered," murmured Victoria. She smiled. "Poor old Bentley!" Her shoulders shook.

"It's not funny, Mummy."

Victoria wiped her eyes. "Granny tried to get him, you know. She chased him round and round the fish pool. He locked himself in the toolshed. He was there for hours. Murdered! Granny *would* be pleased. How did you do it, darling?"

"Well, I can't swear to it, but I don't believe I did."

"Of course you did, my sweet! Have the M'Naghten Rules been amended yet?"

"Mummy, what shall I do about Hugh?"

Victoria looked bored. "Put on your most becoming dress, have your hair waved, and throw yourself upon his bosom."

"You mean ...?"

"You must confess," said Victoria impatiently. "It's only fair. I used to tell your father when I so much as swatted a fly."

"Should I tell Uncle George?"

Victoria did not answer this. When she lost interest in a topic she simply changed the subject. "Tell me, my love," she said, "what is all this about wingless chickens?"

That evening, Hugh Chandor did not go home, but went straight to the

Carp. He needed a drink before he saw Sukie. The saloon bar was deserted except for Alistair Starke, who was sitting on the stairs sketching Mossop. Hugh saw him and tried to sneak back into the mews. Alistair was too quick for him. He shot across the bar, gripped Hugh by the elbow, and led him back, to the counter.

"You're going to buy me a gin-and-French," he said calmly.

"You buy your own drinks," growled Hugh.

"I really don't feel up to it, *amigo*. Not after last night."

Hugh glared. "I see," he said contemptuously. "Extortion. A misdemeanor punishable with two years' imprisonment. Now take your silly face away before I hit it."

Alistair stroked his beard. "Naughty bad!" he said. "That would be a breach of the peace."

Hugh clenched his fists. "That is an understatement. It would be an Affray."

"Climb down, cock. Buy me a drink. Or else."

Hugh ground his teeth and ordered the drinks. Mr. Tooley wobbled them across the counter. He eyed the gin-and-French and mentally reserved half of it for himself.

At 7.30, when Alistair and Mr. Tooley had between them consumed four drinks at Hugh's expense, Sukie came in with George Heap. The latter had visited his niece, ostensibly to inquire about his sister's health. In reality, he wanted to inquire about Mr. Bentley and to have another look at the bomb site, to which he had taken a rare fancy.

Sukie had decided to take Victoria's advice. She had curled her hair and was dressed to confess. She hurried over to Hugh. "Are you still mad at me?" she asked.

"Yes," said Hugh.

"Tell me, young man," said George Heap to Alistair, "has my friend Bentley been in tonight?"

"No sir," said Alistair. "He's given up drinking."

Miles Tate-Grahame came in. He came over to Sukie and bared his long teeth at her. "Thank you so much for the socks," he said. "They're just what I wanted."

Hugh looked up. "What socks?"

Sukie scowled at Miles. To confess to murder was one thing; to admit that one had spent most of the housekeeping money on blackmail was trying any husband too far. "No socks," she said firmly.

"*What socks?*"

Behind Sukie, Miles raised his uneven shoulders and spread his hands apologetically.

"You keep out of this!" roared Hugh.

The Great Tabora rushed in, waving an evening paper. He was flushed with excitement. His cloak was askew and his top hat on the back of his head. He spread the paper on the counter, jabbed his finger at a photograph. "Get a load of this!" he said.

The picture showed him standing with raised whip over a new grave. Tabora was seen in profile. The effect was spoiled only by the fact that his one visible eye was glaring straight into the camera. Further down the page was a picture of Mrs. Pickett washing the steps of the local cinema.

Mrs. Filby beamed. "Fancy!" she said. "Two o' my customers!"

*Three*, Sukie corrected her mentally, looking at the mound of earth over which Tabora was standing.

*Three*, George Heap told himself, concealing a smile. The headline read STRANGLER STILL AT LARGE. He forgave Mrs. Filby her mistake. There was after all no photograph of him, thank God.

From the Ladies' Bar, where the same paper was circulating, came screeches of pleasure.

"Why din 'e take it from in front?" bawled Mae.

" 'Ips, 'ips, 'ips 'ooray!" yelled Lil. "Why did you 'unch yerself up, ducks?"

"Because," said Doris Pickett with quiet pride, "all the fuss made It drop again."

Five minutes later, the best bitter ran out. The brass nozzle coughed, spat out a jet of foam, then blew a large iridescent bubble. Mr. Tooley immediately volunteered to go down to the cellar and change the feed to a new barrel.

"Well, keep your 'ands to yourself then," said Mrs. Filby grudgingly. "An' don't you come back with no funny stories, neither."

Mr. Tooley trotted happily into the kitchen to fetch the torch. *What'll you 'ave, Tooley?* he thought. *I'll 'ave a rum, Tooley, ta. That's a boy, Tooley – 'ave two rums. All right, Tooley, don't mind if I do.*

He scuttled down the steep stairs and flicked the torch's beam unerringly on to the rum bottles on the corner shelf. He broke into a canter. Halfway across the stone floor he tripped over something and went sprawling ...

He sat up, shaken and alarmed. The torch had been flung out of his hand. It had gone out. He could hear it rolling away into a corner. With trembling fingers he fumbled for a box of matches. One of the beer barrels gurgled as Mrs. Filby drew a pint in the bar above. Grunting, Mr. Tooley struck the match. The flame flickered, flared, and settled.

Mr. Tooley sat quite still in the small circle of light. He was unable to move. Slowly his mouth fell open.

Lying comfortably beside him, with her head on one of Mrs. Filby's plush cushions, was Marigold Tossit. Beside her was an axe. She had been hit on the head with it and she was obviously quite dead.

Mr. Tooley knew at once that this was no mirage. Moaning quietly, he staggered to his feet and stumbled upstairs. He shambled into the bar and seized Mrs. Filby's arm.

His superior, who was pouring a brandy for George Heap, promptly spilled it down her bosom. Exasperated, she turned on Mr. Tooley. "Really!" she said angrily. "Some mothers do 'ave them!" She mopped herself down, muttering.

Mr. Tooley jerked his head backwards. "There's another," he said wildly.

Mrs. Filby went red with fury. "You start that again, I'll report you to the brewers," she snapped.

Mr. Tooley raised one foot and stamped feebly. "There is," he insisted.

Mrs. Filby had a moment of doubt. She glanced quickly at her assistant. Misinterpreting his anguished grin, she concluded that he was smiling. "Oh, get away!" she said. She looked at him with loathing and went down to the far end of the bar.

" 'Ere!" Mr. Tooley called after her.

"Oh be quiet!" said Mrs. Filby without turning round.

Confused, Mr. Tooley looked around him for help. Alistair Starke was the nearest. Mr. Tooley shuffled over to him.

"Dead woman in the cellar," he said earnestly.

"You don't say!" said Alistair. "Was she riding a pink elephant?"

Mr. Tooley reached across the counter and snatched at Miles Tate-Grahame's wrist. "Mr. Grahame," he said breathlessly. "Woman dead in the cellar."

"Yes, yes," said Miles impatiently. He brushed off Mr. Tooley's hand and went on telling Alistair how nylon was made.

Mr. Tooley ran around the counter and gripped Miss Dogtinder by the shoulder.

"Remove yourself immediately," snarled the herbalist before he could speak. "You are inebriated. Go on, bunk!"

Mr. Tooley ran on. "Mr. Scales!" he cried.

The undertaker chuckled. "I 'eard you," he said. "Tell it to Macomber an' Pitt."

Mr. Tooley stood still in the middle of the bar. He took his skull in both hands and shook it. Tooley, he asked himself, 'ave you been an' gone an' done it again? He rallied fiercely. No you 'ave not! Was real! He ran over to the Great Tabora.

"Listen," he implored.

Tabora turned his back. "Beat it, hophead," he said callously. He was showing George Heap how to tie knots which never came undone.

Mr. Tooley drooped. He felt a touch on his arm, looked up and saw Sukie watching him sympathetically.

"I know just how you feel," she said. "Who were you going to say it was?"

"S'Miss Tossit," said Mr. Tooley apathetically.

"Coo!" said Sukie. "I wish it was, I mean were."

George Heap leaned across his niece and looked Mr. Tooley between the bloodshot eyes. "Kindly leave us," he said icily. "I find you repulsive and am tempted to strike you." He turned back to the Great Tabora, pulling off his scarf. "I think I've got the Magnus Hitch," he said with barely concealed eagerness. "Now shall we try the Studdingsail Halyard Bend?"

## CHAPTER 8

As soon as Sukie entered her house, she smelled burning. She was standing in the hall sniffing, trying to locate the smell when Hugh came in behind her and slammed the door. He pointed an angry finger at her.

"Now look here, Sukie!" he began. Then he stopped. His nostrils twitched. He pushed past his wife and ran into the kitchen.

Sukie followed him. A small wisp of smoke was curling out of the oven. Hugh jerked open the door. When the smoke had subsided, he peered inside. He turned off the gas and straightened up.

"It's perfectly all right," he said. "I'm doing a spot of cooking."

Sukie looked over his shoulder. There was a small black thing in the oven. One side of it was on fire. Hugh plucked it out with the tongs, held it under the tap, and turned on the water.

"What was it?" asked Sukie when it had stopped hissing.

"It's a roast swede," said Hugh coldly. "I like them crunchy."

Sukie looked at it. It was about the size of a fist. "You've killed it," she said. She drew a deep breath. Here was her opportunity. "Just like I killed Mr. Bentley," she added clearly.

Hugh dropped the swede. It bounced twice and rolled under the sink. He seized his wife by the shoulders. "Say that again," he ordered. "Sukie, look at me! You admit you killed him?"

"That's what I said."

Hugh walked over to the larder, hit the door with his open hand, and walked back again. "Why didn't you say so before?" he demanded. "Why did you lie to me? I knew perfectly well that you'd killed him. Why the hell did you have to insist that you hadn't?"

Sukie hung her head. She watched him from under her eyelashes. She was waiting for an opportunity to throw herself on to his bosom, as Victoria had prescribed, but he was walking up and down and waving his arms.

He hit the table. "I can stand almost everything as long as you don't lie to me," he said. "If you tell me the truth, we know how we stand. If you'd told me at once, we could have got in the police and got you off on a self-defense charge."

"Plea."

"I meant plea. If you do anything appalling, if you feel impelled to kill somebody, for God's sake come to me first and I can advise you. That's what husbands are for. However awful it is, I'll never be angry unless you lie to me. Do you understand?"

"Yes," said Sukie.

"Now tell me the truth. He attacked you, I suppose?"

"Yes. Yes, that's what he did." This, she thought, sounded rather lame, so she added vehemently, "The pig!"

"And you just lashed out at him? You didn't mean to kill him. You got frightened and defended yourself with the nearest thing. It was just an unfortunate coincidence that it happened to be an axe."

"Yes."

Hugh stopped pacing. Sukie stood up, prepared to throw herself into his arms. It was not the right moment. His expression was unfriendly.

"What," he asked, "were you doing with an axe at that time of night?"

"I was – cutting up wood, I was."

"In the dark?"

"Yes," said Sukie firmly. "I always cut it up at night because I can't see when I miss and I don't get nervous."

Hugh frowned. "That wouldn't sound at all well in court."

"But it'll never get to court, darling. They'll never find him. I got away with it." Before he could speak, she rushed on, "I'll never do it again, hand on heart."

"Your grandmother did."

"She was an exception. All the other Heaps are tremendously respectable. Look at Uncle George." She tried to think of another example. Most of the family had something to their discredit. "I mean, just *look* at Uncle George," she said feebly.

Hugh looked at her small, earnest face and held out his hand. "My poor love," he said.

Sukie hurled herself on to his bosom. "Poor me," she said, clinging to him.

Hugh held her away from him. "You swear that you'll never lie to me again?"

Sukie shook her head. "Are you still against me?"

"Well, obviously I'm not delighted."

"But you're not against me?"

It occurred to Hugh that she had been punished enough. She had clearly lied because she had been afraid of him. "I shouldn't have lost my temper," he said. "Are *you* against *me*?"

"Oh, *no!*" said Sukie. "I absolutely love you."

Hugh stroked her hair.

"Ask me how much I love you," she said.

"How much?"

"*Cool million.*"

At 9:40, George Heap, having finished a dinner marred only by another fracas with Tribling, settled by the fire in the club smoking room with the day's newspapers. He was as eager as any actress after a first night to read his notices. In the dailies, he still rated banner headlines, but in the evening editions, he was enraged to note, he had been superseded by a strike at Smithfield Market. Also infuriating was the fact that Detective-Inspector Stoner was playing The Game with such a marked lack of skill. The idiot had now issued a statement that he was working on a theory that the wasteland murders had been gang slayings and had been committed by several different thugs. *Fool!* thought George Heap. *Will I be reduced to sending you anonymous letters?* He looked with distaste at the latest picture of his opponent. *You are a lout*, he told it. *I refuse to associate myself with you. I shall give you not one iota of assistance.* He went into the writing-room and wrote a letter to *The Times* complaining about policemen in general and Inspector Stoner in particular.

At 10:02, Mr. Scales finished embalming an Arab who had tried single-handed to break up a meeting in the Mile End Road, put on a fresh mauve shroud, drank his Ovaltine, and went to bed.

At 10.53, Miss Dogtinder dragged her goat inside her Nissen hut, installed it on a carpet of newspapers, and chained it to the bed.

From 10:54 until 12:08, Hugh Chandor lay staring into the darkness trying to accustom himself to the thought that for better or worse he had married a murderess.

At the same time Miles Tate-Grahame lay awake trying to think out the mechanics of a very small gyrocopter intended for the use of the Flying Squad.

At 12:09, Beecher visited a block of flats in Fulham. He noted that the dead leaf which he had left in the keyhole the day before was still there, and concluded that the tenants were still away. As he had planned, he made entry via the roof, the drainpipe, the balcony. He packed the silver and the furs neatly into a suitcase and left by the front door. He went down in the lift and into a telephone box in the deserted foyer, where he rang up Albert Chivvers and informed him in a falsetto voice that there had been a burglary in Flat 18.

Albert and two plainclothes detectives arrived at the scene of the crime at 1:25. Albert immediately recognized the block of flats as the subject of Beecher's sketch, but he knew better than to say so. Biting his lip, he busied himself with fingerprint powder and magnifying glass. He found only one print. It was a perfect, insolent thumb impression, exactly in the centre of a highly polished table. Almost weeping with rage, Albert watched his superior photographing it. He knew the print was not Beecher's, but he knew equally well that Beecher had put it there.

At 3:07, Mr. Tooley woke with a start, snatched the marmoset off the back of his neck and threw it out of the window.

At 5:19, it began to snow. The chill seeped into the old houses and infiltrated stealthily into every corner. Almost simultaneously, Mrs. Filby, the Great Tabora, and Alistair Starke woke up and shivered. Mrs. Filby got out of bed and put on another pair of bedsocks. Tabora plucked the clammy hot-water bottle from the bottom of the bed and threw it against the wall. Alistair Starke, without opening his eyes, fumbled in the heap of clothes on the floor beside him, found his sweater and pulled it on over his pajamas.

At 7:20, Sukie woke up and lay staring at the ceiling considering herself as an assassin. She was small and slight but she believed that when angered she became taller and could on occasion display extraordinary ferocity. She had the necessary speed and agility. She had, as far as she knew, no previous experience, but the memories of the Heaps were notoriously faulty. Summing up, she concluded that she was a Probable but not a Certainty.

By 8:48, Mrs. Filby had finished sweeping out the bars. She went down to the cellar to fetch the day's supply of spirits and found Marigold Tossit's sad, voluptuous body.

Five minutes later Hugh Chandor snatched his briefcase, kissed Sukie, and hurried off to Lime Tree Court and Mr. Leak, his crammer. Sukie, left alone, headed for the kitchen, where she intended to lick the honey spoon. Taking the bacon rinds into the garden for the birds, she shivered. The snow had not settled properly. A film of it lay on the grass and flower beds, but it had melted on the paths. The water in the earthenware bird bowl had frozen. The bowl had split in half and a semi-sphere of ice lay between the pieces. Hanging the bacon rinds in the pear tree, Sukie tried to remember the last time she had done this. It had been dark. She had laid the torch on the wall, hung up the rinds on this same twig, caught the sleeve of her mackintosh on that briar. She had started back along the crazy paving, turned off the torch because she had the light from the kitchen door to guide her, and then ... The next thing she remembered was standing over a huddled shape by the sundial. She had had something in her hand and had run back into the lighted kitchen to put it on the table. In a confused way she had presumed that it was the torch. Later she realized that it was the axe ...

She found herself staring at a sodden pink vest on the clothesline in the next garden. It was dripping steadily, heavy with melted snow. It was Marigold Tossit's. Marigold! Mr. Tooley had said ... *No!* she thought. *No, not two! I wouldn't have done two! Granny did five, Granny was ... no, she wasn't. She was hanged.*

She darted across the garden, scrambled over the wall, and raced into the kitchen of the Carp.

Mrs. Filby was in there. She was preparing to make some sausage rolls. Her lips were pursed and she was obviously very angry. She pointed the rolling pin at Sukie.

"Yes," she said. "You! I been wantin' to *talk* to you!"

Sukie's heart sank. It was true. "I don't know anything about it," she said.

"Ho no!" said Mrs. Filby angrily. "Now you listen 'ere!"

"I didn't touch her."

"Don't you lie to me! I 'elp you out o' one mess an' then you go an' take advantage!"

"It wasn't me. I've got an alibi."

"Don't you alibi *me*, Mrs. Chandor! You ought to be ashamed to put your 'ead around the door! That's what I get for doin' a kindness! She was one o' my best customers."

"I didn't do it," said Sukie without conviction.

"I shouldn't never of believed you in the first place. Man on a bicycle indeed! I know all about 'Annah 'Eap an' 'er axe. Alibi!"

Sukie was shaken. "Listen," she said.

"I'll give you listen!" Mrs. Filby's hands savaged the pastry dough. "You get out of 'ere an' don't you come back. You're barred, d'you 'ear? Look at the shame! Look at the 'orror! Look at the inconvenience!"

"It was not me," said Sukie loudly. "I can prove it. It was ..."

"That's right," said Mrs. Filby bitterly. "Shift it on to a ninnocent by-stander! I know! *Look out, Mum! Dad's drivin'*!" She stabbed the dough savagely with a fork. "You got to take 'er away," she said fiercely.

"I will not," said Sukie. "She's nothing whatever to do with me."

Mrs. Filby tore a piece off the dough, rolled it into a ball, and hurled it on to the table. "You start that again, I'll send for Albert."

"You can't. You're an accessory after the first fact."

"*Oh* no, I'm not!"

"You are. Ask Hugh."

Mrs. Filby took off her apron and flung it on to the floor. She advanced upon Sukie. "You listen to me," she said with ominous calm. "I'll give you twenty-four hours to shift 'er ... or I don't know what! 'Ave I made my meanin' clear?"

Sukie backed. "Yes. Yes, I'll take her away."

"Twenty-four hours."

"Yes. Yes, all right." She turned and ran out of the room.

She went down to the cellar to look at Marigold. Roarer was down there too. It was too much for her. She raced up the stairs, shot through the kitchen, and ran all the way home.

Mrs. Pickett came out of the larder eating a cold rissole. She did not notice that her employer was pale and out of breath, but plunged straight into her daily bulletin.

" 'Ad a flux last night," she announced with pride. "Bert wasn't 'alf scared! I'm not going to do the stairs today, don't feel up to it. Wouldn't anyway, actual. The Who's 'eard of a *norful* case, I can tell *you!* We 'aven't got the details yet but we're Goin' Slow just to show.

Can only do Light today." She finished the rissole and went back into the pantry.

Sukie went through into the hall and rang up Beecher. In Lupus Street, the receiver was snatched off instantly.

"Hullo," said Sukie. There was no answer. She heard heavy breathing. "Mr. Beecher, please."

Whoever it was started to breathe through his nose.

"Is Mr. Beecher in?"

The breathing stopped as if somebody had put his hand over the mouth-piece, then started again at a different tempo.

"Tell him that it is Mrs. Chandor." She waited.

"Tell him that there has been a complication and will he meet me in half an hour at he'll-know-where."

There was complete silence.

Sukie bit her lip. It was hopeless. Just before she put down the receiver, she heard a muffled guffaw. She recognized it at once. Without any doubt she had been talking to Beecher himself.

Just before noon, Miss Dogtinder left her corrugated home and made for the bomb site. She had in her satchel two packets of marrow seed which she intended to plant behind a screen of giant fennel, rubble, and fireweed. She already had a considerable area under cultivation. Here she imagined, erroneously, that she was unseen and unsuspected. Therefore when she arrived at her allotment it gave her quite a shock to note a large, square footprint near a row of radish, French breakfast.

Filled with foreboding, Miss Dogtinder hurried into the blasted house which served as her conservatory. In the musty drawing room, the tomato plants were untouched. She peered through the service hatch into the dining room. The mushroom bed had not been disturbed. She tramped through into the kitchen. Her mustard and cress still flourished in the disused sink, the *fistulina hepatica* still sprouted serenely from the decaying woodwork, and lungwort which she grew for her chilblains still huddled in the fireplace. Miss Dogtinder was about to turn away when she heard voices.

She stood quite still listening. She was annoyed. The wasteland was hers by Encroachment and yet she doubted whether she could claim Trespass. The voices seemed to be coming from a ruined cellar. Miss Dogtinder tiptoed through the broken glass in the derelict passage and peered down a crumbling staircase.

Sitting on the bottom step and scratching the back of his bull neck, was the man Beecher. With the other hand, he was ripping off and cramming into his mouth pieces of a cauliflower which Miss Dogtinder recognized as one of her Autumn Giants.

Miss Dogtinder ducked back out of sight. She knew Beecher's reputation. She was not exactly afraid of him; she simply did not want to be alone with him anywhere, ever. She imagined that everybody else felt the same way too, and concluded that Beecher, having no confidant and wanting to air his views, was talking to himself. She was therefore considerably startled to hear the slightly hysterical voice of Sukie Chandor.

"But you *must!*" said Sukie wildly. "Because if you don't, *I* can't, and she *will*, and *then* where will we be?"

Miss Dogtinder blinked. She would have liked to ask Sukie to repeat this remarkable question, but she wanted to hear more. The relationship fascinated her.

"*Please*," said Sukie. "Just this once."

The man Beecher grunted.

Miss Dogtinder heard a slight noise behind her. She turned round quickly, clutching her jabot. She had a certain position to maintain in the neighborhood; it would never do for her to be caught eavesdropping.

The cat Mossop was slinking down a derelict staircase. He stopped, immobile, the odalisque eyes trained upon her. He had a dead rat in his mouth. His comfortable old body looked lean, tigerish. Miss Dogtinder was profoundly disturbed. So Mossop too was leading a double life! She flapped her hands at him. He gave her a glance of yellow scorn, then shot past her without a sound. Miss Dogtinder was somehow more shaken by the cat's duplicity than by the fact that the delicate, charming Sukie Chandor was clearly a burglar's moll. From human beings she expected treachery, from animals never. For the first time, she wondered whether her goat was deceiving her. This thought drove all others from her head. She hurried from the blasted house and sought out her darling.

The goat was yearning towards the poster on the hoarding. This had been changed. It now showed Tyrone Power standing on the poop of a galleon and waving a sword. The bottom left-hand corner was torn. Tyrone Power's right foot was missing. The goat's eyes slid around to Miss Dogtinder.

"Joan!" called Miss Dogtinder. "Come, Joan!"

For a moment Joan did not move. Her satanic glance raked her mistress. Then she turned away and rubbed her horns on the struts of the hoarding.

Miss Dogtinder comforted herself that it was the weather. *I shall treat her perfectly normally*, she thought. *Let* her *make it up*. She sniffed, adjusted her hairpins, and retired. As she squeezed through the gap in the railings, she saw Senator standing behind a yew tree. He, too, looked at her without trust.

Miss Dogtinder crossed the cobbles and made for the haven of the Carp. Mossop, old and homely, lay on top of the Guinness barrel. He opened one eye and stared at Miss Dogtinder. She went into the saloon bar and sank gratefully on to a settee. She was deeply troubled.

Alistair Starke, who was at the bar talking to Albert Chivvers, looked at her inquisitively. *Something here*, he thought. *Wild-eyed. Mad as a snake. What have I got on her?*

Albert did not turn round. "Oh, *I* dunno," he was saying. "Makes me wild! Lions! If it 'ad been anybody 'cept Mrs. Chandor, I wouldn't of taken no notice."

Alistair took off his sandal and picked a stone from between his toes. "Has anybody else seen it?" he asked maliciously, having heard of Miss Dogtinder's *faux pas*.

Albert jerked his head backwards.

Alistair looked at him sharply. How did the man know that Miss Dogtinder was behind him?

Albert looked at him sideways and grinned. "We 'ad another report, too," he said. "Nasty piece o' work known to the Force as Lights. 'E saw it standin' in Battersea Park an' gazin' at the river. It looked depressed, 'e said. He wondered whether it was contemplatin' suicide. I ask you! Ain't 'e a joker?"

"Lot o' fanciful nonsense!" said Mrs. Filby from the far end of the bar. While Roarer and Marigold were still in residence she wished that Albert would use another House.

Alistair spun round. Her tone had been diffident. She knew! Mrs. Filby glared back with equal hostility. She realized with misgiving that Alistair was on to her. She also realized, with a surge of impotent wrath, that he intended to profit from his knowledge.

"I will have a large gin-and-French," he said, confirming her fears.

"They ring up over all sorts," said Albert sourly. "Ghosts, poltergeists, monsters in the river. Last week we 'ad one 'oo'd seen a flyin' saucer. We 'ave to check up. 'S'routine."

Mrs. Filby banged Alistair's drink down on the counter. "Four an' free," she said without hope.

Alistair smiled. "I'll have this one with you," he said kindly.

"Know somethin'?" asked Albert, kicking at the brass rail. "British public's s'posed to be the most law-abidin' in the world. Know what I think? I think that's a lot o' malarkey. I think there's a drop o' loony in us all. Takes the wrong set o' circs to bring it out. Might 'appen to anybody.

Plus or minus, you might say." He realized that he was talking too much. *Cor!* he thought. *On two milds an' I 'ad an egg for breakfast!* "Well," he said, putting on his armband, "I must get back to the beat. If a lion clonks in 'ere an' asks for twenty Players, give us a ring." He looked resentfully at Miss Dogtinder, clapped on his helmet, and marched away.

Mrs. Filby, red with rage, leaned over the counter and scowled at Alistair. "Now you look 'ere," she began.

Alistair raised his eyebrows. He made an eloquent gesture with his thumb towards Miss Dogtinder.

Mrs. Filby bit her lip. "Oh, 'ow I *'ate* you!" she said in a grating whisper. Her voice rose with suppressed passion. "*Why don't you never cut your toenails?*" Her face was pinched with rage. She turned on Miss Dogtinder. "And what can I do for you, madam?" she growled. "Or 'ave you come in for a nice rest?"

## CHAPTER 9

HUGH CHANDOR came into the saloon bar just after one o'clock and looked around for his wife. Except for the Great Tabora and Miles Tate-Grahame, the bar was empty. These two were in a corner, sparring in their classic manner. Each was determined to have his say.

"I told that dame over and over," Tabora was saying, "that the wire was frayed. 'Don't be dumb,' I said. 'Use the net.'"

"Quite," said Miles. "It only goes to confirm what I am attempting to say. The incidence of cretins in the British Isles is one in thirty. One in ten is completely ineducable. Psychiatrists ..."

"Yair, yair, yair," said Tabora impatiently, "That dame was nuts all right. Does she use the net? No sir! She grimps up the ladder, opens her damfool parasol ..."

"Quite. She was asking for it. What I am asking for is the nationalization ..."

"And what happens?"

"... of psychiatrists. Every adult should be conscripted into a period of analysis, after which ..."

"Just like I said. *Smackeroo!*"

Hugh went over to the bar. Mr. Tooley was washing glasses in the sink under the counter.

"Have you seen my wife?" asked Hugh.

63

"No," said Mr. Tooley. "I got a fork, though."

"Wife," said Hugh loudly.

Mrs. Filby marched over, polishing a glass. "Don't you shout in 'ere," she ordered. "You want to shout, you go up to Marble Arch."

"Have you seen Sukie?"

Mrs. Filby replaced the glass among its brothers. "Don't you talk to me 'bout *that* young woman!" she said over her shoulder. "I've 'ad enough of 'er, thank you very much. She's barred."

"Why?"

"She's a nice little thing, but she's gone too far."

Hugh swallowed. He should have known that Sukie would not be able to keep her secret. "Oh," he said helplessly. "She told you."

"She did not. I went to get the gin an' I found 'er."

Hugh rubbed his cheek. "Gin? Where did you find her?"

Mrs. Filby leaned across the counter and looked around to see whether anybody was listening. She lowered her voice. "Cellar. 'Ead on the cushion Eunice gave me." She scratched her head irritably. "Mr. Bentley I could stomach. But Miss Tossit, *no!* 'E only came in twice a year, but she was a regular."

Hugh clutched at the counter. He had gone very pale. "Marigold?" he said, "Oh, no, not another! You mean ...?"

Mrs. Filby was amazed. "Mean to say she doesn't *tell* you?" she asked incredulously.

Hugh pinched the bridge of his nose. "You're drunk," he said dully.

Mrs. Filby bridled. "You don't talk to me like that," she said quivering. "Fed up with both of you, I am. You and your wife an' 'er axes!" She noted Hugh's pallor. " 'Ere!" she said anxiously, "you need a drink."

"Axe?"

" 'S'right." Mrs. Filby looked at him. " 'Ave a gin on me."

Hugh turned and ran out into the mews. The door banged behind him. Tabora and Miles Tate-Grahame looked up startled.

In the sudden silence, a voice was raised in the Ladies' Bar. "I got a dog," it said, "an' two cats."

Beecher, who did not believe in paying for anything unless it was absolutely unavoidable, dropped nimbly off his still-moving taxi exactly opposite the restaurant where he intended to have lunch. He shouldered open the door and went in. Several of the customers looked at him with well-bred distaste.

Solly and Lights had already arrived. They were sitting at a table for four. Solly was cutting a piece from a newspaper with a razor blade, and

Lights was making a bird out of the menu. They did not look up as Beecher sat down.

" 'Ere!" Beecher summoned a waiter.

The waiter looked at the trio and curled his Greek lip.

"Loop the loop, three," said Beecher. The man hesitated. "Go on, *go on*!" said Beecher, his voice rising.

The waiter went hurriedly. Beecher turned his attention to Lights.

"I 'ear from ole Flash Chivvers," he jeered, "as 'ow you see a lion larst night."

"Ar," said Lights without rancor. He twitched expertly at the menu and the bird became a Bonaparte hat. "That made me be in Battersea, see? They pull me in 's'mornin' an' I was needin' a somewhere else."

The Queue came in. His hair was newly washed and he wore a remarkable green suit. He threw himself into a chair and took off his shoes. "Heaven!" he sighed. "My plates have been quite, quite killing me." He rubbed his insteps together. "Shoes ought to be *illegal*. If I were king, I'd make everybody wear little knitted bags." He pointed at the hovering waiter. "You! Run and get some Champers."

Solly did not like the Queue. The latter was a scion of a wealthy family and had taken to crime on a whim. He had also taken to it like a duck to water. He was a better burglar than Solly. Solly therefore missed no opportunity of expressing his disapproval. "You talk too much wit your face," he said.

The Queue ignored this. "I suppose you know that they've nicked the Strangler? Finger told me. It's a pug, all strong and sweaty. Ouf! He's at the Station helping the busies with their inquiries, tee hee. We all know what *that* means."

The waiter brought the soup. The Queue pinched his arm. "What about *me*?" he said shrilly. "Ask *me* if I want soup."

The waiter bent over him. "Sir?"

"Well, I don't, so there!" said the Queue spitefully. "You can take your silly little soup and throw it on the floor."

"Ar *shuddup*!" ordered Beecher. He snatched a handful of bread and pressed it into his soup.

The wine waiter, behind Solly, released the cork of the champagne with a loud plop. Solly's hand leapt to his shoulder holster. Beecher kicked him under the table. Solly glared at the waiter.

"Very comical," he said. "Har har."

"I shall have steak," announced the Queue. "Great big steak rare as rare can be."

The waiters left raising their eyebrows at each other.

"What the Chandor skirt want?" asked Lights.

"Got another stiff," said Beecher, his mouth full.

"You goin' to accommodate 'er?"

"Might as well."

"Turnin' soft, Boss?" asked Solly.

Beecher did not speak. He picked up a knife and tapped Solly's soup plate with it. The plate broke neatly in half and the soup spread across the cloth. A passing waiter rushed to attend to the mess. The four watched him in silence. When he had finished, he went away, looking back amazed.

"Wot you goin' to do wit this one?" asked Lights.

"Lose it on a bomb site. No need to do any diggin'. 'Ump it into a blarsted cellar, lean on one o' them crummy old walls, an' nip off quick."

Solly was still mopping himself down. "S'pose you *know* wot you done to me lap?" he inquired quite bitterly.

Nobody took any notice of him.

"Think she did 'em?" Lights had once seen Sukie and, although he would never have admitted it, had taken an immediate fancy to her.

"Dunno," said Beecher. "Might of. 'Er old Granny done in five."

The steaks arrived. The Queue slapped his with a spoon. "That's not rare," he complained. "It's quite, quite *raw*. I don't believe it's even dead. It's just *hurt*." The waiter removed the plate. The Queue seized his wrist. "You put that back at once!" he shrilled. "Go away and get me some Escoffier sauce, you idiotic creature."

The waiter retired looking heavy.

"Young to 'ang, ain't she?" remarked Lights.

Beecher reached out and took a tureen of gravy from a passing tray. He did it so quickly that the waiter did not notice.

"Know wot I'd do if I was you?" asked Lights.

"I want your advice, I'll ask for it," growled Beecher.

"All right," said Lights aggressively. "All ruddy right!" He speared a potato and dropped it back on to his plate with a splash.

"Don't *do* that you dirty pig!" screamed the Queue. "Just *look* what you've done to my tie!"

The people at the surrounding tables sat back to watch.

"Know wot you can do wit your tie?" inquired Lights.

The Queue stood up. "I'm going *straight* home," he said. "I've never been so insulted in all my life!"

"Siddown!" roared Beecher.

The Queue closed his eyes and stuck out his chin. Beecher stood up and moved his shoulders. The Queue sat down quickly.

Beecher turned to Lights. "Well? *Wot* would you do if you was me which you ain't an' never will be?"

Lights looked crafty. "I'd shift the suspicion," he said.

" 'Ark at 'im!" jeered Beecher. " 'E'd shift the suspicion! Ain't 'e a wonder?"

"You don't want my advice, you don't ask for it," said Lights, annoyed. He rolled a piece of bread into a gray pellet and flicked it offensively into Beecher's food.

Without looking up, Beecher reached his knife across the table and pushed over Lights' glass of wine. "Arright," he said. " 'Ow would you shift the suspicion, you talkin' marvel?"

"Go rub yerself down wit a bag o' soot," said Lights.

"Come on, *come on*." Beecher clicked his hairy fingers irritably.

"Spose you never 'eard of a plant?" asked Lights sarcastically.

Beecher sneered. "Oh, so it's a plant, is it? Misleadin' clues, is it? Ain't 'e a ruddy miracle?"

The waiter slid up to remove the plates. The Queue pointed a fork at him.

"You!" he said. "Ask me if I want coffee."

The waiter pretended that he had not heard and hurried away.

"We care for this joint?" asked Beecher softly.

The four looked around appraisingly.

"Na," said Solly. "Tablecloths is dirty."

Beecher nodded. When the waiter returned with the bill, Beecher handed him a five-pound note and accepted thirty shillings change. The waiter hovered, waiting without real hope for the tip. Beecher, with lordly gesture, gave him a pound. The waiter's face split into a broad smile. Eagerly he helped Beecher into his discolored Burberry. He escorted the quartet to the door and bowed them out. Around the corner, Beecher uncurled his hand, smoothed out the five-pound note, and replaced it in his wallet.

"Cost 'im four pound, that lot," he remarked with satisfaction.

Hugh Chandor, having run all the way home from the Carp, found his wife in the drawing room darning socks. She looked up guiltily.

"I didn't do it," she said at once.

Hugh clenched his fists. "I want you to understand", he said, "that I'm not angry. *I'm absolutely bloody well, blind hopping furious!*"

Sukie swallowed. "Yes, but you see ..."

"If you're going to start lying again, I shall hand you straight over to Albert."

Sukie clutched at his jacket. "It was an Excusable Manslaughter."

Hugh brushed her off. "There is no such thing!" he shouted. He opened the window, put his head outside and drew several deep breaths. When he came back, he was still flushed but his tone was calmer. "Do you realize," he said, "that I have spent the last five years learning how to trap and convict people just like you? Do you appreciate the enormity of what I am doing? I am an officer of the Law. Do you understand that I am *committing a crime*!"

"So are all my other accessories. I've got five now."

"Be quiet!"

Sukie watched him. He began to pace up and down the room.

"Two!" he said. He knocked his fists against his temples. Sukie's mad logic was contagious. "I must keep calm, I must keep calm." He drew back his foot to kick a chair, then put it carefully back on to the floor. "Why did you have to do *two*? Why the hell couldn't you leave well alone? Bentley wasn't so bad. We could have claimed self defense. But now you really *have* fixed it. I can't see a loophole. No jury in the world would believe that Marigold had attacked you." He ran a hand distractedly through his hair. "What are we going to *do*?"

Sukie was slightly comforted. He was still on her side. "It's all right, darling," she said eagerly. "I've got an arrangement with Mr. Beecher."

Hugh kicked the chair. "I forbid you to have anything more to do with Beecher!" he roared. "*Why did you do it*? And don't lie to me or I'll send for Albert."

Sukie looked hunted. "All right," she said. "Yes, I see. You mean why did I do it?"

"What did Marigold ever do to you?"

"She did."

"Did what? I don't understand you."

"She threatened me."

"What with?"

"With acid."

"You're lying."

"Oh no. She had it in her bag in a little bottle. She was going to throw it at me."

"Why?"

"I expect she was in love with you."

"She was not and you know it."

"Well, that's what she said. So I sprang at her and strangled her."

"You hit her on the head with an axe and we both know it."

Sukie did not answer. Hugh sat down and put his head into his hands.

*She's not crazy*, he thought, *but I wish there was some simple test to prove it to me.*

"What am I going to do with you?" he said desperately. "Do you realize that if I don't get through this exam, we shall probably starve? How can I concentrate if every time my back's turned you go off and kill somebody?"

"I'll never do it again," said Sukie.

"That's what you said last time."

The Great Tabora passed the window, homeward bound. He was not entirely sober and was walking with one foot in the gutter and the other on the pavement to prove to himself that he was not drunk. He looked in at the window and saw Sukie. He doffed his top hat with a flourish. Sukie waved.

"Stop waving your arms about!" shouted Hugh. He walked up to the wall and banged his head on it. "Why *me*?" he roared. "Why does it have to happen to *me*?"

His wife pushed her darning under a cushion and stood up. She squared her shoulders. "I'm going to phone up Uncle George," she said.

"Oh no you're not!"

"I am," said Sukie. "We're all muddled up. We want someone with new perspectives. He won't approve, but he's Family. It's like Granny used to say. 'In hour of need, run at speed, quickly leap for the nearest Heap.'"

## CHAPTER 10

GEORGE HEAP sat in the club smoking room and studied the lunchtime edition of an evening paper. He looked again at the picture of Basher Adams. The wrestler had been detained while loitering for insufficient reasons around the scene of the Strangler's latest achievement. He was now at Scotland Yard being questioned. The police had issued no statement.

George Heap frowned. Was this genuine stupidity on the part of Inspector Stoner, or was it a fiendishly multiple bluff? George Heap did not believe in underestimating an opponent. He was convinced that the Force – with the possible exception of Inspector Stoner and the louts on point duty – was a shrewd, relentless army of vast cunning. With years of arduous training and every device of modern science behind them, they were a formidable enemy. But the Stoner brute was displaying no imagination, no finesse, no humor. He had apparently not appreciated the exquisite clumsiness of the crime and had detained a punch-drunk member of the working classes. Was this move a blunder, a gambit, or a deliberate insult?

Sipping his coffee, staring at the moronic, halftone features of the wrestler, he vowed that unless the man were released before the final editions, he would strike again. He could not let an innocent man be humiliated in his place; it was not cricket. Anyway, it seemed imperative to reassert his personality. The Yard must be forced to play The Game. This lack of inspired opposition was dispiriting. He glanced at his watch. He still had several hours before he need make his plans for the evening. If Adams were freed, he would dine early and later play a game of bridge; if the wretch were still in custody, then the thrice-tested machinery of murder would slide smoothly into action. The victim and the locale were already selected. In the absence of Mr. Bentley, Tribling was to cease on the bomb site in Wharf Mews.

George Heap sighed. He realized that even murder was losing its challenge. He made a conscious effort to become interested in the details of the crime, but found it impossible. There was little danger in premeditated murder without motive. He sighed again at the intolerable boredom of existence and wandered out into the hall.

Tribling was there, reading a notice on the board. He was perched on his fat little legs and, as usual, snuffling into a handkerchief. His colds lasted all the winter.

George Heap approached him silently from behind. What was the man reading? The menu for the lunch he had just eaten? The menu for dinner which he must already know by heart? George Heap looked over his enemy's shoulder. Except for the menus and the bridge schedules, the only reading matter was a column of donations by members to the club staff. Tribling's name headed this list. His donation was still the largest.

George Heap felt a sudden spasm of rage. He stepped back a pace and appraised his *bête noire*'s neck. The carotids were flabby, the thyroid cartilage looked bent. He was speculating upon the condition of the trachea when the porter approached him, looked at him curiously, and informed him that he was wanted on the telephone.

Tribling turned and met George Heap's pale eyes. For a second the two looked unsmilingly at each other, then Tribling blew his nose, turned back to the notice board, and wrote his name on the bridge list. George Heap touched his mustache with the tip of a finger. It would not be long before he put an end once and for all to the man's despicable underbidding. He went into the telephone booth, picked up the receiver, and announced himself.

His niece's small, clear voice told him that she had to see him immediately. It was a matter of life and death.

George Heap knew Sukie's talent for exaggeration. He did not hurry. Emerging from the revolving door, he stopped to buy a fresh gardenia for his buttonhole and a late edition of the *Star*. He slid into the Buick and opened the paper on the steering wheel.

The front-page headline concerned another strike at Euston. The Stop Press commented that there had been another smash-and-grab raid on a West End jeweler. In a two-inch column on page three was the statement that Basher Adams had been arrested. He had been formally charged with being in possession of nineteen identity cards.

George Heap inclined his head. Tribling's cold would not bother him for much longer.

Hugh Chandor had given up trying to dissuade his wife from confiding in her uncle. She was a Heap. It was no use arguing with her. He showed George Heap silently into the drawing room and withdrew. At least he did not have to hear Sukie confess again to a double murder.

He sat gloomily in the kitchen and watched the light fade outside. He wondered briefly whether the Strangler had a wife and whether she felt as he did himself about her partner's dangerous hobby.

Sitting still, he listened to and yet tried not to hear the murmur of voices on the far side of the wall. At every minute he expected a cry or a bellow of rage as Sukie broke the news. He wondered whether George Heap would faint. He sat waiting for the man to rush into the hall to phone for the police. The moments dragged by. Nothing happened. There was only the drone of the two voices and the tinkle of teacups.

He could not have known that Sukie's uncle's principal reaction to the story he had just heard was intense annoyance. George Heap was biting his lip. He was not greatly surprised that Sukie had committed homicide. Most of the Heaps had done so at one time or another. A casual acquaintance would not have thought that his niece had either the physique or the inclination for such vehemence, but a connoisseur of the family would have remarked Sukie's uncanny resemblance to Hannah and held his peace. George Heap struggled to control his expression. That his niece had accounted for two, only one less than his own bag, piqued him. That she had selected Mr. Bentley, the only man in the world he really yearned to strangle, was intolerable. He bit savagely into a sandwich.

In the waning light Sukie could not see him clearly. "You're taking it jolly calmly," she said. "I thought you'd be *livid*." A moment later she realized that this was premature.

71

"I am furious," said George Heap. His voice was expressionless. He stared out of the window at the wasteland. "Did he struggle much?"

Sukie rose and looked down at him. She saw the vein throbbing in his temple. "You look most odd," she said anxiously. "Would you like an aspirin?"

George Heap had not heard her. "Why," he demanded, "do you summon me now, when the man's death is a *fait accompli*? Why did you not ask my advice *before* taking this step?"

Sukie too gazed out at the bomb site. The snow had flattened the fireweed. Quilts of it lay along the shattered walls. "I don't remember," she said. She sighed, depressed. "I hardly remember anything. It wouldn't have made any difference. You know us Heaps. You can't talk us out of things."

George Heap turned suddenly, his fine eyes flashing. "I would have restrained you, if necessary, by *force*." His voice broke with suppressed rage. He closed his eyes and cleared his throat.

Sukie took the sandwich from his nerveless fingers. "Honestly," she said, "you'd better have an aspirin."

George Heap passed a hand over his hair and straightened his tie. "Tell me," he said, "do you intend to make a habit of these lapses?"

"Oh *no!* At least, not if I can help it."

Her uncle sipped his tea. He looked better now. "You are wise," he said coldly. "Temperamentally, you are unsuited to such activities. I absolutely forbid you to do it again."

"I didn't intend to do it ever. I think it's awful."

"Moreover, your methods are repellent."

"They were good enough for Granny." As soon as she had said this, Sukie regretted her lack of tact. She knew that both George Heap and Victoria owed their lives to the fact that they could run faster than Hannah.

George Heap did not comment. They sat for a moment in silence. Before both of them rose the image of Hannah as she was represented in Madame Tussaud's. Hannah of the charming smile, the tiny feet, the organdy sunbonnet. The bunch of parma violets tucked into the belt, the bloodstained axe hidden shyly behind the voluminous skirts. George Heap shuddered. Sukie dropped the sugar tongs and the spell was broken.

"What are we going to do?" she asked.

Her uncle lit a cigar and blew a funnel of smoke. "*We*?" he said, affronted. "You suggest that *I* should implicate myself in so brutish an imbroglio!"

Sukie looked up quickly. "You've *got* to help," she said indignantly. "It's Family. Don't you remember? 'United we stand, we fall in a heap.' "

72

George Heap pulled irritably at the lobe of his ear. "At the moment I have commitments of my own. What do you expect *me* to do?"

"I thought you might think up a new angle, so to speak. We're all rather bogged down."

George Heap brushed ash off his lapel. "I will think it over," he said. "Tomorrow. This evening I have a previous engagement."

"Do you think", asked Sukie, "that we could palm her off on the Strangler?"

George Heap turned away his head and ground out his cigar. "No," he said carefully. "I don't believe we could."

Sukie studied him. In the half-light she could see only his handsome profile silhouetted against the window. "For a moment," she said uncertainly, "I thought that you were laughing. Would you like another cucumber sandwich?"

George Heap left soon after. As soon as the car had purred away, Sukie hurried to the telephone and dialed the Lupus Street number. It rang for some time and Sukie, knowing that this was not normal, was about to ring off when a waspish voice said in her ear, "All right, all *right!* What *now?*"

"Can I speak to Mr. Beecher please?"

"No, you can't," said the Queue. "He's out."

"Is Mr. Lights in?"

"You can't speak to him either. He's making chutney."

"I would like to leave a message for Mr. Beecher. Will you tell him to hold everything until he hears from me? It's very important. There's been a new accomplice."

"I went to see your old Granny this afternoon," said the Queue for no apparent reason.

"Oh? How is she?"

"All right. Bit dusty."

"Will you remember to give my message to Mr. Beecher?"

"I really couldn't say." The Queue sneezed and rang off.

Hugh came out of the kitchen. He looked at Sukie, ran a hand through his hair, and went into the dining room. Sukie followed him. He slumped into a chair and stared into the fire. She studied his harrowed face and was tactfully silent. She took her notebook from her pocket and after doing several small sums found that she could just afford to pay her accessories out of the housekeeping money.

Beecher had been thinking. By seven o'clock, he had considered Lights' suggestion about diverting suspicion and decided that it had possibilities.

He therefore went along to the Carp with the intention of collecting a few false clues. His motives were mainly malicious, but he also realized that if Sukie were arrested and hanged, he would not get the considerable sum of money she had promised him as soon as she could afford it. Anyway, the distribution of spurious evidence would not only madden Albert Chivvers, but also impede Law and Order generally, which in itself was always desirable.

Having made up his mind not to incriminate any of his drinking companions in the Public, he made for the Saloon.

Mrs. Filby was the daughter of a boilermaker's assistant and had worked for her living since she was ten years old. Her heart was with the Labour party but she regularly voted Conservative. She had passionate opinions upon the segregation of different classes. The internal economy of her public house depended upon these profound taboos and her convictions were reinforced by the very architecture of the place. There was a right position for everybody, both in the Carp and in Mrs. Filby's philosophy. She could tell at a glance and with great acumen the social status of new customers. They were directed gently but firmly into the bars which befitted them. The discovery of water snakes in the best bitter would have dismayed Mrs. Filby far less than the presence of an Earl in the Public; and this evening, Beecher's excursion into the Saloon almost deprived her of speech.

"Get back where you belong!" she croaked. "Go on! *Disappear!*"

Beecher surged over to the counter. "You speak?" he inquired.

Mrs. Filby paled. "You 'eard!" she said angrily.

Beecher spat out a splinter of chewed match. "Yus," he agreed. He leaned across the counter making his shoulders ominous. "Go on, *go on!*"

Mrs. Filby's courage was exhausted. She went. Pale with rage, she drew the pint of rough cider. She nudged the barrel, hoping to stir up the sediment and ruin the man's drink, but the ruse did not succeed. Luck, as usual, was on Beecher's side. The burglar snatched the tankard, lifted his lip at Mrs. Filby and paid in coppers. He then went and sat on a settee next to Miss Dogtinder. The herbalist, outraged, rose immediately, averting her eyes.

"Please 'elp me," whined Beecher. "I got tennis elbow."

Miss Dogtinder hesitated. She was interested in spite of herself. Moreover she knew that her Nissen hut would be simplicity itself for Beecher to ransack. "Indeed?" she said warily. She did not want to be seen speaking to the man and she dreaded his weird aroma. The healer in her tussled with her disgust. The healer, as usual, won by a short head. She sat down.

"Figwort," she said. "*Knotted* figwort. The leaves crushed into a paste with hog's lard." She, like Miles Tate-Grahame, could never resist imparting useless information, so she added casually, "Venus owns the herb and the Celestial Bull will not deny it." She did not notice that Beecher's hand was in her pocket. "It is also efficacious for wens, kernels, and bunches."

There was nothing in her pocket except a bag of shelled nuts. Beecher put it back and turned his attention to her handbag.

There was a heavy pause. Miss Dogtinder moved her long feet nervously. "When is your birthday?" she asked, unable to endure the silence.

"Chooseday," said Beecher gruffly. He was not going to admit that he knew neither the date of his birth nor his age. He got his hand into the woman's bag and felt around swiftly.

"Ah!" said Miss Dogtinder. "Sagittarius. The moon is now in its fourth quarter. You will have a disappointment on Sunday."

Beecher sucked his teeth. He decided to postpone the Knightsbridge job until Monday. His roving hand found a small sachet. He drew it to the mouth of the bag and without moving his head glanced down at it. It was mauve muslin and it had Y.D. embroidered on it in green. He jerked it up his sleeve and slid his hand out of the bag. Miss Dogtinder had not noticed. She was holding her head back and turned away from him. His object achieved, Beecher rose, mooched over to the bar, and eyed his next victim. Alistair Starke stared back at him. He was not afraid of Beecher. He had nothing worth stealing. Briefly, he wondered whether it was any use trying to blackmail the man.

"And where were *you* last night when the lights went out?" he murmured.

Beecher looked at him with scorn. "You want yer 'ouse mucked up?" he asked. He flexed his hands on the counter.

Alistair tried a laugh. "Only joking," he said quickly.

Beecher thought fast. He did not quite know what to take from the man. A handkerchief would have been suitable, but none of Alistair's would sport a laundry mark. He washed them himself and ironed them by flattening them on his window panes. A tube of paint from the studio might have done, but Beecher simply could not be bothered to go and fetch it. He could have picked the pockets and tried his luck, had the artist not got his hands in them. It would have to be a piece of material. Alistair was wearing a pair of rust-colored corduroy trousers. Beecher opened the small blade of the penknife in his pocket. He looked around to see whether he was observed. Miss Dogtinder was reading a seed catalogue. Mr. Tooley and Mrs. Filby were behind the bar. Mr. Tooley was sharpening a pencil, Mrs. Filby was watching Beecher in the mirror. This did not worry the burglar. The piece of Alistair's trousers he hankered for was below the level of the counter, out of her range of vision. He moved around behind the artist.

"Don't push, you great oaf," said Alistair crossly.

Beecher moved away. " 'Ere!" he called Mr. Tooley.

Mr. Tooley shuffled over, grunting. He was talking to himself under his breath. Beecher heard the word Panda.

"Pint of 'It Me Once," he ordered.

"Don't you call me no names!" said Mr. Tooley. He flushed angrily. "You know what you are an' you can keep the change!" He did not feel Beecher take the pencil expertly out of his hand. He tossed his old head and stalked away. He went down to the far end of the bar and, still glowering, went on sharpening the pencil which was no longer there.

Beecher carved the letters T.T. on the pencil and dropped it into his pocket. He looked around for new victims. He considered Mrs. Filby. She was sturdy and she had great big bones, but she was an unlikely murderess. Beecher did not want to implicate everybody, merely to spread a little confusion and to provide Sukie's defense counsel, should she be arrested, with one or two damaging items against the other suspects. He was still pondering when Miles Tate-Grahame hurried in and, as he always did, peered around shortsightedly for somebody who would listen to him.

"Good evening," he said tentatively to Miss Dogtinder.

The herbalist recognized the gambit. She knew that if she so much as answered his greeting, he would settle beside her and methodically proceed to bore her into a torpor. She rose. "Good evening," she said. "I was just leaving." She gulped down her gin and tonic, choked, bowed, and departed patting herself on the chest.

Miles spotted Alistair. "Ah, Starke," he said. "Here's something which may interest you." He opened his hand and disclosed a small test tube. It was full of a colorless liquid and at the bottom was a tiny green culture.

Beecher looked at it and wanted it immediately.

Four minutes later, everybody in the saloon bar, including Beecher, was searching for it.

It was during this search that the Great Tabora arrived. He flung open the door with his customary flourish and inadvisedly allowed it to swing back on to Beecher's crustacean fingers. The housebreaker, who had been pretending to peer behind the weighing machine, stood up with a muffled oath. Pursing his squashed lips, he went to Tabora and tapped him on the shoulder.

"You 'urt my 'and," he said.

Tabora looked at him disdainfully. He did not know the man's profession but he took an instant dislike to his cap. "Tough," he said coldly.

Beecher sucked his teeth. "Yore goin' to regret this, cock," he said softly.

Tabora stuck out his under lip. "Go spit up a rope," he said rashly. He turned his back.

Beecher studied the cloak's imitation astrakhan collar for a moment while he decided how to punish its owner. He stood nursing his injured hand. His mood deteriorated. Suddenly he saw how he could cause Tabora a great deal trouble. It was risky, it was against his orders, but as a revenge it was perfect. He headed for the passage. He was about to start down the steep stairs to the cellar when Mrs. Filby opened the hatch at the back of the bar.

" 'Ere!" she called. "Where d'you think you're goin'?"

"You was the one 'oo wanted 'aulage an' cartage. Twenty-four hours, you said."

"Oh," said Mrs. Filby. "Well, keep your 'ands to yourself. Only one thing in that cellar I won't miss an' don't you forget it."

Beecher went down the stairs. He turned on his torch and stood it on a barrel. Somebody had covered Marigold Tossit with an old curtain. Beecher pushed Roarer into a corner and arranged his false clues in prominent positions. Immediately he opened Miles Tate-Grahame's test tube, there was a puff of foul smoke and the culture disappeared. Beecher dropped the test tube on the ground and carefully trod on it. He then looked around the scene of the crime and wondered whether he had overdone it. Miss Dogtinder's sachet lay at the foot of the stairs, Mr. Tooley's pencil by the barrels, the broken test tube nearby, and the piece of Alistair's trousers hooked onto a splinter on the bottom step. If the police came here, they would undoubtedly find a wealth of microscopic clues like hair and dust. The larger items would stand out like sore thumbs. Beecher made a quick decision. He picked up Mr. Tooley's pencil and put it back into his pocket. To counterbalance this move, he promoted the piece of corduroy to the hand rail, where it showed more. Satisfied, he scooped up Marigold and crept quietly back upstairs. There was nobody in the passage nor the kitchen. It was nearly closing time. Only Tabora and Miles Tate-Grahame remained in the Saloon. In the Public, a man was singing "All Things Bright And Beautiful".

Beecher let himself out of the back door into the dark yard. He felt his way along the wall and climbed over into Marigold's garden. He passed within a foot of Miss Dogtinder's Nissen hut. It was in darkness. For a moment he thought that he detected a movement behind the curtains and then decided that he had imagined it. As he ducked into the shadows of the house, it began to rain. He slung Marigold over his shoulder and opened the back door with his chain wrench.

Inside the house, he crept through the dark hall. The quiet business gentleman who rented the front room was playing the *Harry Lime Theme* on a very old gramophone and singing lustily. Zithers hurt Beecher's teeth. He put a corner of his handkerchief into his mouth and bit on it. He waited until the man turned over the record and began to play the other side before he turned on his torch and stole upstairs. The house was in darkness. He flashed his torch into two rooms before he was satisfied that he had found the right one. He smiled. With an exhilarating feeling of power, he laid Marigold Tossit on the threshold of the Great Tabora's bed-sitting-room.

"Two spades," said Tribling proudly. He snuffled in the significant manner which every bridge player in the club knew to mean that he had at least four and a half honor tricks.

"Pass."

"Three no trumps," said George Heap.

"Pass."

Tribling paled. He hated forcing bids. He dropped a card, clapped a plump little paw over it, and shuffled it clumsily back into his hand. He gave George Heap a look of hatred, blushed, and said, "Pass."

George Heap drummed his fingers on the table.

Masterman grinned. "Double," he said with relish.

"Five clubs," said George Heap. He stared at Tribling's buccinator. It had been an idiotic error to allow the man this last game of cards, but it had been raining at the scheduled starting time.

"Pass."

Tribling did not look up but he knew that they were all watching. Masterman was despising him. Cloon was embarrassed for him. George Heap could have murdered him. He laid his cards down on the table and, to gain time, blew his nose. The soles of his feet were tingling. He tensed the muscles of his calves and one of his suspenders came undone. In his panic, it seemed to him imperative that his sock should not fall down. He tried to hold it up with his other foot. He had no idea what to bid. He suspected that George Heap had mentioned clubs solely to confuse him. Had the fellow got any clubs or was he trying to confide that he had only one ace? Was he playing Culbertson or Blackwood or some new swine that Tribling had never heard of?

"Hurry it up, old chap," said Masterman.

"Take your time," said Cloon.

Tribling's sock fell down. He lost his head. He intended to pass, but to his horror he heard himself bid seven no trumps.

There was a moment of silence. George Heap's face twitched. Masterman was overcome by a fit of coughing. Cloon bit his lip. Tribling picked up his cards and put them into his pocket. Masterman doubled. George Heap played the hand with an expressionless face. The only indication of his displeasure was a pulse throbbing visibly in his right temple.

By common consent, they settled up at the end of the game. Masterman and Cloon accepted their checks and rose immediately. Both were eager to get away from the scene of Tribling's crime.

The offender, not wanting to be left alone with his partner, also rose and half-ran upstairs. George Heap followed him. He arrived at the end of the passage just in time to see Tribling scuttle into the bathroom at the far end with a book under his arm. He strode silently along the corridor and listened outside the bathroom door. A few minutes later he heard a splash and a sigh as the waters received Tribling. He knew that the man would be there for at least two hours. Fuming, frustrated, he phoned down to the porter and told him to garage the Buick. He had changed his plans and would not be going out again that night.

## CHAPTER 11

It was nearly midnight by the time Mrs. Filby and Mr. Tooley had finished washing up the glasses and emptying the drip pans back into their respective barrels. While Mrs. Filby counted the take, Mr. Tooley padded out into the kitchen and found a cold fish cake. He ate a piece of it, grimacing. He did not want it; but he did want a legitimate excuse to remain downstairs until Mrs. Filby had gone up to bed. His superior knew exactly what he was thinking. A little while later, she came into the kitchen and stood just inside the door watching him.

"Peckish," said Mr. Tooley. He held up the fish cake.

Mrs. Filby said nothing. She stared for some time at a framed aquatint of the Battle of Jena, then turned on her heel and marched out of the room.

Mr. Tooley listened, his jaw suspended. He heard her climbing upstairs. He counted the footsteps. Eighteen. Mr. Tooley had occasion to know that there were twenty-one steps. He snatched another fish cake, sat down at the table, and pretended to be reading the *Morning Advertiser*.

The door banged back against the wall as Mrs. Filby burst into the room. Mr. Tooley, suppressing a leer, looked up mildly. Mrs. Filby, outwitted, angrily cleared her throat. They regarded each other.

"Goin' to a fire?" inquired Mr. Tooley.

Mrs. Filby sniffed. "All right," she said. "You win. But don't think I don't *know*."

This time she genuinely went upstairs. Mr. Tooley heard her banging about in the room overhead. He threw the fish cake out of the window, snatched a candle, and nipped down to the cellar. Contentedly drinking rum, he eyed Roarer and tittered. *Larns!* he thought. *You're a card, Tooley, an' no mistake! Whatever will you be seein' next?*

Fifteen minutes after midnight, the Great Tabora turned off the kitchen light in Marigold Tossit's house, tucked his hot-water bottle under his arm, and went yawning up to bed.

The quiet business gentleman in the front room was snoring loudly but otherwise the little house was in complete silence. On the half-landing above, Tabora turned on the light. He had been whistling soundlessly through his teeth. He stopped abruptly. One foot remained poised above the first step of the upward flight. He dropped the hot-water bottle.

Lying across the doorway of his room was Marigold Tossit. Her eyes, on the same level as his own, were surprised and resentful. She was very obviously dead.

Tabora stood quite still. He had in his time seen several violent deaths. He was more surprised than horrified. For a moment he wondered at his lack of awe. He remembered the horror with which he had seen a trapeze artist deliberately miss his wife as she hurtled through the air towards him. That incident, he supposed, had somehow immunized him. He had watched his best friend misfired by a faulty cannon into the audience with nothing more than a vague nostalgia. When, a week later, an elephant had sat upon its trainer, he felt only a mild irritation that the beast had done so at a matinee. Death had lost its sting for Tabora.

The hot-water bottle slid slowly off the top step, flopped on to the next one and, gathering momentum, rolled down the whole flight. A door was snatched open downstairs.

"Less noise up there!" bawled the quiet business gentleman. "How can a chap sleep?"

Tabora thought fast. He realized instantly that he was in an extremely compromising position. He also knew that the man downstairs disliked all Americans on principle and would delight in seeing one arrested for murder.

"Sorry, brother," he called. "Won't happen again."

The other went grumbling back into his room and slammed the door. Tabora took Marigold by the legs and towed her into his room. He sat down in a basket chair and poured himself four fingers of whisky. Gulping, he leaned back and shut his eyes. Mr. Tooley's image swam up under his eyelids. "Dead woman in cellar," it said earnestly. "Woman dead in the cellar."

Tabora took hold of the end of his mustache and twisted it. So it was a frame, was it? Somebody was playing Bright Boy, was he? Trying to pull a fast one on Tabora, was he? On *Tabora*, who knew every shady trick from Cardiff to K2! The lion tamer laughed mirthlessly. He stood up and jerked down his tunic. He would show this dim wit that he was no fall guy. Purposefully, he picked up the body and slung it over his shoulder. He turned off the landing light and peered downstairs. The quiet business gentleman was asleep. He was grinding his teeth.

Tabora did not like it, he did not like it at all. But from the point of view of the police a body in one's bedroom was worth two on a bomb site. He hitched Marigold a little higher and started very warily downstairs.

Seventeen minutes after midnight, the front doorbell rang in the Chandors' house. Five minutes later, Hugh plucked up the courage to go and investigate. He was convinced that it was the police, that they had come to arrest his wife and charge himself with being an accessory after the fact. He spent four, frantic, whispering moments coaching Sukie in what to say when she was charged, then went slowly downstairs. Reaching the bottom step, he looked back over his shoulder and saw his wife's small, frightened face hanging over the banisters.

"Have you got it straight?" he hissed.

"Yes," breathed Sukie. " 'I am absolutely not guilty.' "

"What else?"

" 'You are making a terrible mistake. I want my lawyer.' "

"Then what?"

"I cry."

"And if that doesn't go down well?"

"Faint."

"And if they revive you?"

"Faint again. Go on and on fainting until they're bored stiff."

"All right. Go back to bed and collapse."

"Already?"

"Go on."

Sukie vanished. Hugh heard her bare feet pattering into the bedroom and the protest of the springs as she leaped into bed. He drew a deep breath, straightened his shoulders, and flung open the door.

There was nobody there.

A thick ground mist lay along the narrow road. The tips of the railings, variously colored and bright under the street lamps, poked through it like small furled flags. The snow lay melting in the gutters. Moisture dripped steadily off the eaves. For a moment Hugh had the uncanny feeling that an army of policemen was advancing silently under the mist.

"Hullo!" he called. His voice was muffled. He waited, feeling that at least there ought to be an echo, but there was none.

He went back into his house, shut the door, and leaned against it. He was surprised to find that he was slightly out of breath. Sukie's head popped inquiringly around the banisters at the head of the stairs.

"There's nobody there," said Hugh. He rubbed the back of his neck.

"I think I'm going to be sick," said Sukie.

"If you're sick, I really will lose my temper." For no reason he wiped his feet briskly on the doormat. His left foot skidded and he looked down puzzled.

He was standing on a postcard. It was addressed to himself in crude block letters. He picked it up and turned it over. Written in the same illiterate hand was the legend YORE OLE WOMAN AS LEFT CLUES ALL OVER THE BOOZER. FRIEND.

Hugh smacked himself in the forehead. "Sukie!" he said. "Oh God! Did you leave any clues?"

Sukie sat down abruptly on the top step. "Crikey!" she said. "I'd forgotten all about clues!"

"Think, think hard. Did you leave any in the Carp?"

"I don't remember. I don't remember any of it."

Hugh struggled into his overcoat. Sukie ran downstairs and put on her mackintosh.

"Where are we going?" she asked.

"Over to the pub to check up."

"We'd better wear scarves. It's jolly cold out there."

"You're not coming."

"Yes, I am. *Why* aren't I?"

"Because I say so."

"I don't see why I should stay at home while you have all the glory."

Hugh did up his belt and rolled up the legs of his pajamas. "You've done quite enough," he said.

"I'm not getting anything except the ignominy."

"You are not coming."

Sukie looked at him. He meant it. "Well anyway," she said resigned, "do up your top button."

Hugh left her in the hall. He found a pair of brogues in the kitchen and put them on. He collected a box of matches and, not knowing what to expect in the way of clues, Sukie's shopping basket.

As he let himself out of the back door, the mist swirled around him. There was no moon and the sky was overcast, but the mist had its own eerie radiance. There was no sign of life in the surrounding houses, but again he had the feeling that he was being watched. He marched boldly across the garden swinging the basket. He wondered whether to whistle nonchalantly but decided against it. As he climbed over the wall between his own house and the Carp, the basket became entangled in the branches of a pear tree and he had to climb back to unhitch it. He tore it loose and a shower of half-melted snow descended upon him. Swearing, he shook himself and climbed over the wall again. He decided that in future he would wear a more suitable outfit for these midnight expeditions. The blouse of his battle-dress, for instance, and perhaps an old pair of plus-fours. Glancing up at Mrs. Filby's dark windows, he wondered how she would react if she knew that he was about to break into her premises. Probably she would not bat an eyelid. She had taken two murders in her stride; she had even volunteered to be an accessory. That this was a criminal offence did not appear to worry her unduly. She would not have dreamed of playing cards on Sunday or reading other people's letters, but she had with apparent alacrity committed Compounding, Conspiracy, Receiving, and several forms of Felony. She had her own idea of right and wrong.

As he approached the back door, Hugh thought he saw a large, flat face pressed against the window. He hesitated, wondering what explanation he would give if he were caught. He watched paralyzed as the kitchen door opened slowly inwards. Then he saw that the man in the doorway was Beecher and clenched his hands.

"I'm getting fed up with you," he said in a furious whisper. "Don't you ever go home?"

Beecher jerked his head backwards and made an impatient gesture with his hand. Hugh gave him a startled look and pushed past him into the kitchen.

There was a candle in the middle of the table dripping slowly into a saucer. Beyond it on the wall was a monstrous crouching shadow and in between the two, sitting hunched in a wooden chair, was the Great Tabora. He was gagged and bound and there was an ugly bruise on his forehead. He inclined his head eloquently towards Hugh and worked his eyebrows. Beside him on the floor lay Marigold Tossit in an advanced stage of *rigor mortis*.

Hugh tried to say something but his voice had disappeared. *Actual Bodily Harm*, he thought absurdly. *An assault calculated to interfere with the health and comfort of the aggrieved.* He shut his eyes and pinched the bridge of his nose.

Beecher sloped past him and patted Tabora on the head. The lion tamer flinched, expecting more violence. Beecher watched him, drumming his fingers on the man's skull with something like affection.

" 'E wants 'is lawyer," he said fondly. *"Doesn't* 'e?" He slapped Tabora lightly on the back of the neck and hurried out of the room.

Hugh stood at a loss. He glanced uncertainly at Tabora. The man tried desperately to speak. He made a strangled noise and frowned heavily, shaking his head. Hugh made a movement towards him and stopped. *That damned lion*, he thought, *is still in the cellar. If Tabora sees it, he will exhume the coffin and Sukie will be charged with* two *murders.* Tabora made a stupendous effort and jumped the chair a few inches forward.

"Yes," said Hugh. "Yes. I know just how you feel. But – well – take it easy. I'll be right back." He looked into Tabora's anguished eyes and wondered which of them felt the worse. "I'm awfully sorry," he added lamely. He nodded encouragingly and set out after Beecher.

There was a light in the cellar. Hugh went down the stairs two at a time. Beecher had set his torch on an upturned barrel. The cone of light lit up a dank patch on the ceiling but otherwise the place was in semidarkness. In the shadows, the burglar was helping himself to gin. Hugh snatched the bottle from him and replaced it on the shelf with a bang.

"Do you realize what you've done?" he demanded. "That man is now a material witness."

Beecher wiped his mouth on the back of his hand. He picked up the torch and flashed it on Roarer. "You want 'im to see old 'airy face?" he inquired. "You want yer other stiff back? That the idea?"

Hugh put his hands into his pockets and took them out again. "What difference does it make?" he said hopelessly. "He's seen Marigold."

Beecher leered. " 'E won't sing," he said confidently. " 'E thinks we got the idea 'e done 'er in. 'Snot right to get caught with a stiff 'angin' around yer neck like a ruddy muffler. 'Snot legal."

Hugh sat down on the stairs and tugged at his hair. Beecher walked about pulling faces. His boots crunched on the stone floor.

"Stand still, for God's sake, man," said Hugh hoarsely. "I'm trying to think." He looked up suddenly. "Did you write to me?" he asked.

"Can read too," said Beecher noncommittally.

Hugh, remembering why he was there, looked around him. He saw Miss Dogtinder's sachet. He turned it over with his foot and stared at the initials. "What on earth would she be doing down here?" he muttered.

"Murderin'," said Beecher.

Hugh kicked at the sachet. "Please don't try to confuse the issue," he said coldly.

Beecher found a wine gum in his pocket. He detached a piece of fluff from it, rubbed it on his sleeve, and put it into his mouth. " 'Nother clue right beside you," he observed. He directed the torch on to the scrap of corduroy caught on the hand rail.

Hugh looked at him suspiciously. "How did you know it was there?"

"Saw it."

Hugh fingered it. "Starke's got a pair of corduroy trousers," he remarked.

Beecher was bored with the business of the clues. He wanted to get back upstairs and molest Tabora again. He stepped backwards on to the crushed test tube.

"What's that?" asked Hugh sharply.

"Dunno." Beecher kicked at it, carefully missing it. Hugh returned to the corduroy.

"Felt like glass," said Beecher. He shone the torch on it.

Hugh looked at it, stiffened, and stood up. "Do you know what I think?" he asked slowly.

"Wot?"

"I think that there are too many clues."

"Go on," said Beecher uneasily. "Take that 'Urley case. Two 'undred an' fifteen exhibits, 'undred an' four witnesses."

"What are you doing with your feet?"

"Shufflin'," said Beecher. He demonstrated.

There was a crash from upstairs. Hugh took the flight in three bounds. Beecher snatched up the clues and followed him. In the kitchen, Tabora, still lashed to the chair, had fallen over. Mossop was stalking around him, sniffing at him curiously. Tabora was straining to get away from him. He hated small cats. Overhead, Mrs. Filby banged on the floor.

"Shuddup!" bellowed Beecher.

There was silence. Mrs. Filby had recognized the voice. Beecher picked up Tabora and patted his shoulder.

"Me an' this genius wants to be alone," he said. "We're goin' to 'ave a little parley."

Hugh shuddered. "What about?" he said quickly.

" 'Im."

"Anybody else?"

"Go on," said Beecher. "*Fade.*"

Hugh hesitated. He avoided Tabora's rolling eyes. He did not like to leave the man alone with Beecher, but short of attacking the burglar, he saw no immediate alternative. Bleakly, he comforted himself that Beecher had never yet committed murder. Feeling guilty, he left Tabora to his fate. Beecher caught him at the door and pushed the basket of clues into his hand.

Crossing the yard, Hugh saw that there was a light in Miles Tate-Grahame's laboratory. He wondered what the man could be doing at this time of night; whether the regulars of the Carp had always behaved in such an extraordinary manner and only now, after two murders, had he noticed it. He wondered whether any or all of them were mad; whether most people had, so to speak, a lion in their cellars and remained undetected until some calamity brought them more clearly into focus. As he climbed over the wall, Miles Tate-Grahame came out of his laboratory and peered around shortsightedly.

"Who's that?" he called.

Hugh, waist high in mist, stopped in the ray of light from the open door. "Me," he said savagely. "Around this time of night, it's always me."

"Oh," said Miles. Puzzled, he eyed the basket. "Picking mushrooms?"

"Whatever you say," said Hugh. He was past caring what Miles thought.

He went into his kitchen, put the basket on the table, and sat down on a chair. After a moment he rose, picked up a saucepan, and hurled it on to the floor. It clattered away into a corner. Hugh, unappeased, went after it and kicked it. He heard Sukie's bare feet running along the passage, turned his back, and stared out of the window.

Sukie burst into the room and stood blinking in the glare of the light. She noted the bent saucepan and the set of her husband's shoulders and stopped dead.

"Would you like some Horlicks?" she asked carefully.

Hugh did not answer.

"Are you still against me?"

"Yes."

Sukie poured herself a glass of milk and drank it. When she had finished it, she asked, "Why?"

Hugh drummed his fingers on the window pane. "I'd rather not discuss it."

Sukie's curiosity overcame her discretion. "Didn't you get any?" she asked.

"Any what?"

"Clues."

Hugh dragged a hand over his face. "I'd rather you didn't mention that word," he said distantly.

Sukie saw the basket. She pulled it towards her and looked into it. She had never before, as far as she knew, seen a clue. She clapped her hands.

"You *did*!" she said enthusiastically. "Well *done*, darling! They're *beauties*!"

## CHAPTER 12

THE next morning the snow had almost disappeared. On the roofs, a few patches still clung but they were thawing fast, dripping steadily down the tiles. The roads were wet and shining, the gutters full of sodden leaves. There was not a breath of wind and the smoke from the chimneys rose straight towards the leaden sky. In the dim, sullen light, the little painted houses around Wharf Mews looked garish, slightly unreal.

Shortly after eight o'clock, Albert Chivvers, bound for the local police station, passed the Chandors' house on his bicycle. He looked up and rang his bell. Sukie bobbed up at the bedroom window. She waved. Albert nodded and pedaled slowly on, his tires hissing through the puddles. He was sorry that he had been unable to wave back but decorum forbade it. Around the corner, he dismounted with the slow pavane the Force had taught him and blew his nose.

Miles Tate-Grahame came out of the side door of his house holding a letter. He saw Albert and bared his long teeth.

"Morning, constable," he said. "Have I done anything?"

"Dunno," said Albert. " 'Ave you?" he added hopefully.

"Not that I know of. Caught any more lions?"

"Barmy," said Albert. "You got a radio?"

"Yes. Why?"

"Got a license?"

"I'm afraid so. Sorry."

"Oh well," said Albert. "No 'arm in askin'. You get fed up with nippers on roller skates. No trouble with the neighbors? Nobody makin' a pest? Nothin' at all?"

"No. It's a quiet district."

"Routine, routine, routine," said Albert, kicking at his tires. "Pal o' mine gets on 'is first big case in twenty-four years. Know what 'appens? 'E gets shot."

Miles walked down the road towards the pillar box. Albert walked along beside him.

"Heard any more about the Strangler?"

"Wasn't that Basher Adams. 'Is 'ands didn't fit. They'll get 'im. Somebody else will. Not me."

"Well," said Miles, "where there's death, there's hope." He shook with laughter.

Albert was not amused. "Proper browned off," he said.

Miles wiped his eyes. "I must remember to tell that to Starke," he said. "Where there's death, there's hope."

Albert looked at him with dislike, got laboriously on to his bicycle, and rode away.

At 8.30, Alistair Starke stormed into the Chandors' kitchen by way of the back door. He had dressed hurriedly. One pajama leg protruded from the bottom of his dirty flannels and his beard was rumpled. Sukie was at the stove wearing Hugh's dressing-gown and frying bacon.

"Where were you last night?" Alistair demanded.

"Here." Sukie did not turn round.

"Prove it."

"Oh go away!"

Alistair took the frying pan out of her hand and banged it down on the table. "Let me tell you, young woman," he said violently, "that you're not going to get away with it! This time you've outsmarted yourself!"

Hugh came into the room. He had *Criminal Law in a Nutshell* open in his hand and was obviously learning something by heart. He saw Alistair and scowled.

"You get out of here," he said aggressively.

"Where were you last night?"

"Lower your voice, you cheap crook."

"Where were you?"

"Mind your own business."

Sukie dished up the bacon, put it on a tray, and carried it out of the room. Hugh looked Alistair up and down turned on his heel and followed his wife into the dining room, locking the door behind him.

Alistair went out of the front door and climbed in through the dining-room window.

Hugh came around the table and caught him roughly by the shoulder. "Look here, Starke," he said. "I've had just about enough of you."

"Put me down," said Alistair angrily. "I'm not leaving until I find out which of you did it."

Hugh let him go. "Did what?"

Alistair breathed hard through his nose. "Put Marigold Tossit in my hall."

There was a pause.

"No," said Hugh with sudden determination. "No! I've had enough. Count me out." He marched out of the room and banged the door. A moment later the front door slammed.

"I expect it was Beecher," said Sukie, frowning. "I must speak to him. I told him distinctly to lose her on the bomb site."

Alistair stared. "I think you're mad," he said.

Sukie poured another cup of coffee and pushed it across the table. "If I tell you something, will you swear not to tell Hugh?"

Alistair was incurably inquisitive. "All right," he said.

"*Well.*" Sukie beckoned him to come closer. "I'm not at all sure I killed them," she whispered. "At first I wondered whether I'd had an amnesia. Our family does, you know. But I don't believe I'd forget *both* of them, do you?"

Alistair tapped a spoon on his saucer. "I don't know and I don't care," he said. "You damn well tell your lout of a henchman to get that body out of my house."

Sukie stirred her coffee. "I bet Albert would like to know about that," she said. "He's dying to find a corpse."

Alistair looked up sharply. "Oh no you don't!" he said. "If you set Albert on to me, I'll spill the beans."

"No you won't. You'd hate jug."

"All right," said Alistair after a heavy pause. "You've made your point. What do you want?"

"I want you to help me question the other suspects."

· Alistair raised his eyebrows and looked out of the window. "You *are* mad," he said.

Sukie produced a small writing pad from her dressing-gown pocket. She ripped off the top sheet and tore it in half, giving one half to Alistair. "That's your lot," she said.

Alistair looked at it. It read: *Mrs. Filby, Mr. Tooley, Miles Tate-Gra-hame, Miss Dogtinder, Me.* He frowned.

89

"It's quite fair," said Sukie. "I've got Mr. Scales, Mr. Tabora, Hugh, Beecher, and you. Five each."

Alistair sighed. "Even if we presume that it wasn't you, how do you know it was any of *them*?"

"I don't. I just hope so. Where were you on Tuesday evening? What is your alibi?"

"Don't be absurd! Why should *I* want an alibi?"

Sukie looked at him sideways and wrote something on her sheet of paper. "What was your motive?"

"I didn't have a motive. I didn't do it. *You* did. What are you writing?"

"*Motive – Don't know*."

"What do you mean *Don't know*? I tell you I hadn't got one. Put *None*."

"You must have one. If you kill people without one, you're mad."

"I have not killed anybody," said Alistair clearly.

"Prove it. Where were you on Wednesday evening?"

"In the local. I was with Hugh and I can prove it."

"You needn't look so jolly smug. We don't know what time she was killed so you've got to have an alibi all day long."

"There's no such thing."

"Yes, there is. You could have been out of the country. You could have been up in an airplane. You could have been in plaster of Paris."

"Well, I wasn't."

"Exactly. What was your relationship with the deceaseds?"

"Bentley once bought me a drink. Periodically I took Marigold to the cinema and held her hand. What are you writing?"

"*Motive – Jealousy*."

Alistair hit the table with his fist. "What do you mean *Jealousy*? I was not jealous. I didn't care a hoot about her."

Sukie studied him, crossed out what she had written, and jotted down something else. Alistair watched her suspiciously.

"What have you put now?"

"*Motive – Hatred*."

"Now look," said Alistair. He spoke slowly and distinctly. "I did not love her. I did not hate her. I was not jealous of her. *I did not kill her*."

Sukie was not impressed. "Prove it," she said promptly.

Alistair clutched his beard and strained at it. "No," he said. "*You* prove it."

"All right." Sukie produced the scrap of corduroy which Hugh had found in the cellar of the Carp. "How do you explain this damaging clue?"

Alistair took it. "It's a bit of my trousers!" he shouted. "Some swine's been cutting up my trousers!"

"That," said Sukie, "was found in the cellar with the second deceased. You caught it on the stairs as you bashed her on the head with the axe."

"Axe? What axe? I haven't got an axe."

"I know you haven't. You left it behind and Mrs. Filby's using it now."

Alistair mopped his forehead. "All right," he said. "Have it your own way."

"You confess?"

"No!" roared Alistair. "I do *not* confess! I refuse to confess!"

Sukie folded the piece of paper and put it into her pocket. "Well," she said briskly, "that's the end of my preliminary inquiry. I must of course warn you not to leave the district." She wrote something on a fresh piece of paper and pushed it across the table. "Sign here please."

"What for?"

"What's the use of a statement unless you sign it?"

Alistair took it and looked at it. *Mr. Bentley once bought me a drink*, it read. *I had no alibi and no motive for killing him. I did not love, hate, or care a hoot about Marigold Tossit and I had no motive for killing her either. I refuse to confess.* Alistair scratched his head. Sukie's peculiar sanity had an almost mesmeric effect on him. He hit the paper irritably with the back of his hand. "This is damn silly," he said weakly.

"Of course," said Sukie, nodding. She added in the same tone, "Sign it or I'll fetch Albert."

"You wouldn't dare. You'd be arrested for murder."

"Maybe. But I'd never be hanged. They'd just send me back to Mummy. You see, under the M'Naghten Rules ..."

Two hours later, still ruffled, Alistair sat in the saloon bar of the Carp sipping a gin-and-French. He was furious with himself for signing Sukie's lunatic document, but he had had no alternative. She was apparently unmoved by the thought of arrest; Alistair was not. He bit his thumb at the mere idea of prison. Sukie had an even chance of getting away with it, particularly in view of that ludicrous statement and the body in Alistair's cupboard. There was only one thing to do. To get rid of Marigold at the first possible opportunity and to reduce the statement to an absurdity by tricking or bullying equally damaging admissions out of everybody in the neighborhood. He realized with impotent rage that he too had been drawn into the current of Sukie's mad logic.

It was only just after opening time. So far he was the only customer, but at any moment the door might swing to admit another early drinker. He had got to work fast.

He pointed a dirty finger at Mrs. Filby. "Where," he demanded, "were you on the night of Tuesday last?"

Mrs. Filby looked at him contemptuously. "Why don't you never wear a tie?" she asked. "Ought to be ashamed goin' around like that! Look like a rasher o' wind tied up ugly." She turned away to pour herself a Bass. She had the cap of the bottle under the patent opener before she swung back, her eyes narrowing. "An' what do *you* know 'bout the night o' Tuesday last?"

"I am not trying to implicate you," said Alistair soothingly. "I merely want to establish your alibi."

"On 'oose authority?"

"Mrs. Chandor's."

"*Well*!" said Mrs. Filby. "She's got a nerve!"

"I agree. Where were you on Tuesday?"

" 'Ere."

"Alone?"

"Now an' then."

"Whereabouts?"

" 'Ere an' there."

"You were a friend of the first body's?"

"On an' off." Mrs. Filby tugged absently at her corsets. " 'E fixed up a cat o' mine once. Fair terror, that cat was! Talk 'bout cream passionelles! 'Ad to put 'im down in the end. 'E went on an' *on*."

Mr. Tooley appeared, sucking a cachou. He swayed, clutched at the cash register, which rang up eight and tenpence, and was about to retire when he spotted Alistair's gin-and-French.

"You're drunk!" said Mrs. Filby, outraged.

"Seen any more dead women?" called Alistair.

Mr. Tooley clawed his way along the counter. He shook with silent laughter. "Aren't I *awful*?" he mumbled. He leant forward until his face was within an inch of Mrs. Filby's. "Boo!" he said defiantly. He reached across the bar and gripped Alistair by the sweater. "Was a man, too," he boasted. "Most people never get past lizards, but I'm always doin' it."

Alistair pushed a piece of paper across the counter. "Remarkable," he said. "May I have your autograph?"

Mr. Tooley held the piece of paper at arm's length and squinted at it. Then he laid it down on the counter, backed three paces, shot his cuffs, sprang at the paper, and signed it with a flourish which sent him reeling against a barrel of Guinness.

Mrs. Filby seized him by the collar and shook him.

"Oh, you '*orrible* old man!" she grated.

Mr. Tooley struggled, trying to reach Alistair's drink, but it was just out of range. Mrs. Filby turned him forcibly, aimed him at the door, and propelled him out of the bar. Alistair heard them stumbling upstairs, Mrs. Filby breathing heavily, Mr. Tooley grunting, grumbling, singing snatches of song. There was a slight lull as they reached the landing, a shuffle, a thud, a slap, and then a door slammed. Alistair sat staring after them, amazed for the first time at their curious relationship.

He reached across the counter and helped himself to an outsize gin-and-French. Toasting himself in the mirror, he sat back and reread Mr. Tooley's statement. As the old man's confession had lacked conclusiveness and Mrs. Filby had not signed hers, Alistair had felt justified in uniting them. The result was brief but pertinent. *He went on and on. I had to put him down in the end. Aren't I awful? I'm always doing it. T. Tooley.*

Alistair looked at it with satisfaction. He was no longer alone in his predicament.

Mr. Scales was leading Senator out on to the bomb site. He saw Sukie, raised his bowler hat half an inch, and replaced it. "Mornin'," he said jovially. He patted the horse's flank. "Puttin' 'Imself out to quiet down for this afternoon."

"*Another?*" asked Sukie.

"Some o' them is impromptu. Another o' these 'Idden Culvert cases."

"I see. Where were you on Tuesday evening?"

Mr. Scales beamed. "Drummin' up trade in the Saloon."

Senator stretched his neck, curled back his upper lip, and snapped his teeth. Mr. Scales thumped him.

"Stop that!" he said sharply. Senator looked at him from the whites of his eyes, hacking at the cobbles with his fore feet. "Give 'im an inch," said Mr. Scales significantly.

"Where were you on Wednesday?"

Mr. Scales scratched his nose. "Bad day, that was. We was goin' on a job, but there was what we call a technical 'itch – which means, between you an' me an' this friend o' man, that the old girl pulled through."

Sukie produced a notebook and pencil. "So you had all day to kill?" she asked airily.

"*Cunctando restituit rem,*" remarked Mr. Scales. Then, struck by Sukie's elaborate indifference, he looked at her again. "Why?" he asked doubtfully.

"Just wondering. Would you sign here please?"

"What for?"

"I am taking a census."

"No, I will not," said Mr. Scales flatly. "You ought to be ashamed! An' it's no use givin' me the glad eye, either. I'm old enough to be your Dad.

93

Kindly step aside. My 'orse wants to pass."

"Miss Dogtinder," said Alistair, "you are in quite a spot and I would like to help you."

The herbalist pumped up her Primus stove and stirred the cauldron on top of it with a glass rod. "Bugloss," she explained. "A cordial of the herb imparts tone to the stomach."

"What do you know about Marigold Tossit?" asked Alistair.

Miss Dogtinder lifted a tangle of boiled weeds out of the cauldron and threw them out of the window. "She was destined for a violent end," she said.

Alistair's cigarette broke in half. "You *knew*?"

Miss Dogtinder picked up a spoon and dipped it into the cauldron. It immediately turned black. "I am not a moron," she said impatiently. "When a man carries a girl out of a public house one presumes that she has over-indulged. When another man carries her back, one smells a rat. When she is dropped twice and makes no comment whatever, one assumes that she is either unconscious or dead. When both men behave in a thoroughly shifty manner, one decides that she is dead. One of the men being a ha-bitual criminal, one concludes that she has not died naturally. Q.E.D. Kindly pass me that carton labeled Gromel."

Alistair gave her a hard look. "Why didn't you notify the police?"

"The men in blue," said Miss Dogtinder bitterly, "do not appreciate it when people see things. I once distinctly noticed a lion. The police kept me up all night, implied that I was not myself, and made coarse jests about my goat."

Alistair was slightly nonplussed. He sat down and folded his arms. "I do not intend," he blustered, "to move a muscle until you give me a signed statement about your movements on Wednesday afternoon."

Miss Dogtinder looked at him contemptuously. She sat down at the table, dipped a quill into the ink pot, and began to write. She wrote slowly and used her ruler several times. When eventually she had finished, she blotted the document carefully and handed it to Alistair with a pitying smile.

Alistair grabbed it. Worrying at his cuticles, he read it. The statement had headings, subheadings, an introduction and a conclusion. Every minute of the herbalist's time from Wednesday midday until midnight was ac-counted for. In a separate column, with addresses and telephone num-bers, was a list of witnesses who could corroborate her claims. She had an alibi which even Beecher would have envied.

"No, no," said Alistair involuntarily. "This isn't what I wanted at all!"

Miss Dogtinder got up and banged the lid on to the cauldron. "No," she said. "I didn't intend it to be. Now make yourself scarce!" she barked. "Get out before I lose my wool!"

"Mr. Tabora," said Sukie, "Beecher has told me all about last night. I know everything. *Why did you do it?*"

The small room smelt vaguely of damp cloth, boot polish, whisky, and American cigarettes; but pervading all else was the arrogant, animal smell of Tabora himself. There were two pairs of flashy socks drying over the fender, a packet of Lux on the mantelpiece, an elephant's foot in a corner, a stack of assorted whips, a top hat on a nail behind the door. The lion tamer was ironing his cloak on a card table covered with an army blanket. He had a patch of sticking plaster over one eyebrow and was obviously in a vile temper.

"Can it!" he said tersely. "Don't give me that stuff. I come home, I fix me something to eat, come upstairs, and find her. Some clunk is trying to frame me."

"I suggest," said Sukie grandly, "that this statement is nothing more than the product of your disordered mind."

Tabora scowled. "Dames," he said, "should be obscene and not heard."

"I suggest that whatever you say is a *tissue of lies*. I suggest that whatever you say, the opposite."

Tabora turned the cloak inside out and began to iron the lining. "What do you want?" he asked. "Scratch?"

Sukie considered. "Yes," she said defiantly. "I do want scratch. I want thirty shillings a week payable to Mr. Starke."

Tabora put the iron down and stared at her. The small freckled face was expressionless. "Well, what do you know!" he said, amazed.

"Where did you get the axe?"

"Axe? What axe? I don't get it." Still staring, he scratched his head. His elbow jolted an untidy pile of books on the mantelpiece. The top three fell. Tabora grabbed at the pile but he was too late. The books fell all around him.

Sukie bent to help him pick them up. Tabora liked literature of the bang-bang-kiss-kiss variety. Sukie looked at a picture of a woman with an astounding bosom caressing an icepick. She handed the book to Tabora. "The axe," she prompted.

Tabora flicked the book with his thumb nail. "She doesn't stab' em," he said. "She got some of this poison unknown to science. Axe? Yair, I was axed once. Smyrna. Some smart guy challenges me with strange cats. I try 'em in French, German, and Arabic, but they don't savvy. They speak

Turkish. Wait. Another time, there was, too. Croydon. Roarer throws up in the ring and some mug starts squawking about dope. I bought it then, too."

Sukie passed him a book whose cover showed a giant cactus eating a woman in a bathing suit. "I expect it was quite a blow," she said casually. Tabora shrugged his shoulders. "Could you let me have your signature please?"

Tabora sat back on his heels. It was some time since he had been asked for his autograph. "Sure," he said warmly. "Say, I got you all wrong. You're all right."

Alistair, stamping his feet and blowing on his blue hands, kicked impatiently at the door of Miles Tate-Grahame's laboratory. The inventor loomed up inside. He was wearing an ankle-length rubber overall, gumboots, and a headdress which suggested the Ku Klux Klan. He did not open the door.

"I'm frightfully sorry, old man," he shouted through the glass panels. "You'd better not come in. I'm on to something rather startling. I rather think everything's radioactive."

Sukie rang up Lupus Street. The phone was answered by the Queue, who was in a skittish mood.

"Knock, knock," he said.

"Who's there?" said Sukie, humoring him.

"Me," said the Queue. He screamed with laughter and dropped the receiver. Sukie heard it swinging against a table leg. Presently somebody picked it up.

"Mr. Beecher?"

A breathy silence. Sukie listened carefully and decided that she was speaking to Beecher.

"Just a formality," she said apologetically. "Suppose I didn't do either of them, you didn't either, even if it wasn't me, did you?"

Beecher sorted this out. "Nir," he said.

Alistair went along to the Carp. Sukie was in the saloon bar, sitting on a settee. She was drinking ginger beer, eating potato crisps, and writing in her notebook. Otherwise, except for Mrs. Filby who was down at the far end of the bar doing a shady deal with the local grocer, the pub was empty. Alistair slouched over to Sukie and handed her the two statements he had obtained. She frowned at Miss Dogtinder's alibi and list of witnesses.

"Did you ring them up?" she asked.

"No. I'm broke."

Sukie considered. The housekeeping money was already allocated. She gave Alistair twopence. "I can't afford them all," she said. "Take Mr. Pickering."

"It's a toll call."

"Well, Mrs. Coolsden."

Alistair disappeared into the passage. Sukie got up and sat down nearer to the radiator. Alistair came back and sat down on the settee.

"She won't answer the phone," he said.

"Try this Muir person."

Alistair got up and went back to the telephone. Two minutes later he came back and sat down. "He's out," he said. He helped himself to one of Sukie's potato crisps. "Miles Tate-Grahame wouldn't play."

"Nor would Mr. Scales. It's discouraging, isn't it?"

"What are you writing?"

"Arranging the suspects. I fancy Miles, Tabora, you, Dogtinder, and Scales, in that order."

"Why Miles?"

"He's so awful."

Alistair was cleaning his nails with a pencil. "I fancy you," he said, "in that order."

Sukie ignored this. She handed Alistair another twopence. "Try Mr. Monkton," she said.

Alistair got up and went away. A moment later he came back and sat down again. "He's out too," he said.

George Heap was in an optimistic mood. He had been obliged to make his peace with Tribling; but the latter, flushed with half a bottle of Tio Pepe, had agreed to accompany him that evening to a music hall. Tribling, with an unusual flash of intuition, had wondered for a second whether there were some uncandid motive behind the invitation. His fears, however, had been overruled by George Heap's geniality and the fact that the performance included a Water Spectacle. Tribling loved water.

The Strangler, himself in a mellow mood after several sherries, had for a while seriously considered allowing the fellow to see the Spectacle. After lunch he changed his mind. He climbed into the Buick and went along to familiarize himself with the scene of the crime. He stopped the car some distance before Wharf Mews and walked slowly past the wasteland.

It was ideal. Here were the giant weeds, the camouflage of trailing creepers, the blasted trees; here were the ruined catacombs where a body might lie for several years undetected. It had the air of rank desolation which he had found on these occasions to be so stimulating. Had Mr. Bentley been his prospective prey, he would have been completely satisfied ...

He wondered idly whether Tribling had any enemies. It seemed improbable. Apart from his gaffes at the bridge table, he was harmless enough. It might perhaps be safer to rob him as well, suggesting that the crime had been committed by a ruffian. One could always toss his miserable trinkets into the Thames. This time, George Heap would officially be the last person to see his victim alive. He would undoubtedly be questioned. The Game would require more skill, more daring, more finesse. Perhaps this time he might for a brief spell struggle out of this morass of boredom ...

Then he saw the horse. It was inside a devastated house, watching him through the window. It was black, it was overgrown, it had in its eye the curiously intense regard of an infant prodigy.

George Heap disliked all animals. His mother had fostered in him the belief that they *knew*. Vaguely disturbed, he walked down Cork Street, twirling his cane in a thoughtful manner. He stopped outside his niece's house and rang the bell.

Sukie opened the door and welcomed him with the family formula. "Greetings, Heap! In you leap!"

Her uncle was not in the mood for such pleasantries. He followed her into the drawing room, lit a cigar, and glared out of the window. He could not quite see the bomb site from here. He had not forgotten his niece's dilemma, but his own problems continued to exercise him. It occurred to him suddenly that the Heaps, quite apart from the *noyade* in the Sudan, had accounted for ten lives. He roused himself.

"Have you yet disposed of your second victim?" he asked.

"Not yet. Beecher's going to dump her on the wasteland."

George Heap dropped his cigar. He picked it up and coughed. "That would not be advisable," he said.

Sukie recognized this as an order and was annoyed. "I've made up my mind. It's all arranged."

The Heaps faced each other. Their eyes met. The vein began to beat in George Heap's temple. He was determined not to postpone Tribling's demise for the second time. He was equally determined to have the exclusive use of the bomb site that night.

Sukie stood her ground. Her uncle, she felt, had been extremely unsympathetic about her predicament. Moreover, she disliked being ordered around. She steeled herself to oppose him just for the hell of it.

George Heap knew exactly what she was thinking. Short of violence, there was only one way to deal with her. Gritting his teeth, he forced a smile. He said pleasantly, "Pray silence, Heap. Not a cheep."

In the days of her childhood, in the idiom that her uncle himself had taught her, Sukie had regarded this as the ultimate appeal. She capitulated with good grace. "Well," she said. "That's different."

George Heap made a decision. "You will have this body here by eleven o'clock this evening. *I* shall dispose of it." Seeing that she was about to protest, he raised his hand. "Kindly do not interrupt. I am fully aware that I am doing you a favor. I assure you that my motives are purely selfish. I have worries of my own and I dislike being confused by this inane cabala." He paused and pointed his gloves at her. "You will therefore stop arguing, listen to me carefully, and do exactly as I say."

# CHAPTER 13

MR. TOOLEY awoke from his siesta and clutched his aching head. He realized immediately that his hangover was abnormally severe. Grunting, he got out of bed. There was only one remedy for his anguish. "Come on, you," he ordered the marmoset. " 'Op up." The phantom leapt on to his shoulder and Mr. Tooley went downstairs in search of a drink.

Mrs. Filby heard him coming, darted out, and installed herself at the top of the cellar stairs. She pretended to be examining the paintwork. Mr. Tooley did not see her until it was too late. He changed direction accordingly and went through into the kitchen. Baffled, he stood kicking at the range. He had been outmaneuvered. Mrs. Filby knew.

She came into the room, glanced at him triumphantly, and began to make an omelet for her tea. "Fancy an egg?" she asked maliciously. The hair rose on the back of Mr. Tooley's neck. He turned away and did not answer. *Oh, the beast!* thought Mrs. Filby. "Or there's some cold pork," she added. "Bit fat, though."

"Aou shut up!" snarled Mr. Tooley. He waited until the omelet had reached the critical phase, then nipped out of the room. He scurried through into the bar and grabbed at the rum bottle.

Again he had underestimated Mrs. Filby. "Can I 'elp you?" she asked from behind the hatch. She was slightly out of breath.

Mr. Tooley gave her a murderous glare, replaced the bottle, and shuffled past in a heavy silence. He stood in the doorway until he smelled her omelet burning, then went slowly upstairs. He was not beaten yet. Grunting, he slopped into his room and locked the door. He hauled in the string which led to his cache in the gutter below. Tied on to this lifeline was a bottle of milk.

Mr. Tooley's face twitched. "Very clever," he whispered savagely. "Very clever indeed. So sharp you'll cut yerself." He unlocked the door and shambled across the landing into Mrs. Filby's room. Clawing at the eiderdown, he fell on his knees beside the bed and plunged his hand into the springs underneath. The bottle was still there, strapped exactly as he had left it. He whisked it out, and ran smiling back into his room before he realized that again he had been outwitted. The bottle contained a wooden model of a schooner in full sail.

Mr. Tooley sat down on his bed to review the situation. He was badly frightened. *Tooley*, he thought, *you're a goner*. He sat on his bed for nearly an hour with the ghastly specter of sobriety staring him in the face. Then it occurred to him that he had one more trick up his sleeve.

Miss Dogtinder clumped into the saloon bar just after seven o'clock. She had in her bag a folder of raffle tickets which she intended to sell in aid of a Handicraft Guild of which she was Head Weaver.

The bar was empty except for Mr. Scales, who was sitting in a corner testing the strong ale. Miss Dogtinder bore down upon him. She handed him a ticket and said firmly, "Two bob!"

Mr. Scales was not superstitious. He was first and foremost a business man. The origin and destination of his clients was not his concern. His only interest was their point of departure and their removal from the left hand page of his ledger to the right. To so prosaic a man, Miss Dogtinder had an aura of the Unknown. A mixer of dubious elixirs, a dabbler in astrology and the occult, she also kept a goat, *ecce signum!* He paid up without a murmur.

Miss Dogtinder handed him the folder and indicated the counterfoil. "Sign here, please," she said.

Mr. Scales started. His signature today had been in demand. He had already been approached twice by Sukie Chandor, once by Alistair Starke. There was clearly something odd afoot because the latter had asked him, as man to man, to sign a statement reading *I was drumming up trade*. Mr. Scales had refused on each occasion. He had an instinctive distrust of anything which he did not understand. "No," he told Miss Dogtinder peevishly. "I won't."

For a moment the herbalist was affronted; then the area around her mouth appeared to disintegrate. She was smiling. "Ah ha!" she said. "So he came to you too, the young rapscallion! *I* scotched his snake in a wink."

Sukie came in with the Great Tabora behind her. Tabora made for the bar. Sukie saw Miss Dogtinder bending over Mr. Scales and said quickly, "Cave! He doesn't know."

"Eh?" said Mr. Scales. "*What* don't I know?"

For the first time in her life, Miss Dogtinder had been included in a secret. She found her wrists rearing painfully backwards in the direction of her forearms. This always happened to her in times of social excitement.

Alistair Starke slouched in with Miles Tate-Grahame. Now that Alistair no longer depended upon Miles to keep him in bitter, he treated the inventor with marked coolness. Miss Dogtinder swooped at them with the book of tickets concealed in her hand. Alistair, with the clairvoyant cunning of his kind, slid past her. Miles forced a smile and produced a florin.

"Sign here," said Miss Dogtinder.

Miles stiffened. "No," he said.

Miss Dogtinder took offense immediately. She tossed her head and marched away. Miles and Mr. Scales were left regarding each other covertly. Miles tried to look bored.

"Good evening," he said, "have you any idea what it's all about?"

"No," said Mr. Scales. And after a pause, " 'Ave you?"

"No." Miles fingered his long, gray face. "Has Starke been drinking? He's been dodging around after me all day."

"*Obscurum per obscurius*," murmured Mr. Scales. " 'E want you to sign anythin'?"

Miles looked up quickly. "Not exactly. He said he was studying graphology. He wanted me to write *I was experimenting. The result in each case was positive*."

Mr. Scales pulled at his lower lip. "Somethin's up," he muttered. He leant forward and studied Alistair. The artist was apparently trying to persuade Sukie Chandor to buy him a gin-and-French. Sukie said something in a heated undertone. Mr. Scales strained his ears and distinctly heard Alistair whisper, "Come off it, ducks! What Hugh doesn't know this evening cancels out what you knew this morning."

Mrs. Filby saw the undertaker's expression. "Be quiet!" she said sharply to Alistair. "You want to talk spiv, you go outside."

Behind her back, Mr. Tooley left the bar with a bottle of whisky, an empty ginger ale bottle, and a funnel.

"Attaboy!" shouted Doris Pickett from the Ladies' Bar.

"Aou shut up!" said Mr. Tooley from around the corner.

Miss Dogtinder riffled her tickets at Tabora. The lion tamer disliked

her intensely. She was persistently remarking upon his capacity for alcohol and diagnosing incipient cirrhosis. He bought a ticket with bad grace,
signing the counterfoil in an assumed hand as Tapirbum.

Miss Dogtinder did not notice this. She had already turned her attention to Alistair. "Come on, you young rip!" she said gruffly. "Stump up."

Alistair leapt to his feet. He turned on Sukie. "So!" he said heatedly.
"You double-crossed me!"

"I did not."

"Then how does she know?"

"Who's 'she'?" snapped Miss Dogtinder. "The cat's mother?"

"Don't give her more than thirty bob," murmured Sukie. "That's the
controlled price."

Mr. Scales shot a glance at Miles. "Well, I dunno," he summed up.

Miles kicked testily at the brass rail around the fireplace. "It is a deep
truth," he said sourly, "that the *habitués* of this and most other public
houses are pathological. If one considers that this is a reasonably representative cross-section of the British public, one is forced to the conclusion that we badly need padded cities."

Hugh Chandor came in. With a deep sigh, he sat down on a stool at the
bar and stared at Mrs. Filby. "I thought you'd barred my wife," he said.

"Oh no," said Mrs. Filby comfortably. "Not any more. The cause o'
the ill feelin' 'as been removed."

Mr. Scales looked around him. This was his local. He had been coming here for nearly twelve years. Now and then people had one over the
eight and behaved a bit queer. But never before had he had the spooky
feeling that any of the regulars were madmen; or, with the exception of
Beecher, criminals. Suddenly he had the uneasy suspicion that all of them
were both. He scrutinized each of them in turn.

The man Beecher had materialized from the passage and was muttering in a corner with Sukie Chandor. Why? What could this incongruous
pair have in common? Alistair Starke was sitting on the stairs trying to
overhear their conversation. The Great Tabora was absently ripping strips
off a rubber plant, putting them into his mouth, and blowing them out
again. From the angle of his head, it was obvious that he too was interested in the conversation in the corner. Miss Dogtinder, wearing an expression of extreme cunning, had her thumb and first finger in her mouth.
She was apparently doing something to her teeth. At the same time she
was staring at Beecher. Miles Tate-Grahame was propped against the
mantelpiece watching a fly drowning in his beer. Hugh Chandor was laying out matches on the counter in the shape of a swastika. Mrs. Filby was
motionless behind the bar, wearing the expression of an officer wonder-

ing whether to open fire upon mutinous troops. And Mr. Tooley was drinking ginger ale!

Mr. Scales shut his eyes. He felt the goose-pimples rise on his arms. He had a moment of panic. All these people *knew* something. Why was he the only exception?

Behind him, on the far side of the partition, the inseparable three were conversing in low voices.

"Evil genius, that's what," growled Doris.

" 'E did it all right." That was Mae.

"Only got to look at 'is 'orrible, 'orrible eyes," whispered Lil.

Mr. Scales' blood ran cold. *Whose* eyes? Who were they talking about? *Who?* Would they too stop talking if they knew that he was listening in?

In the Public, the grocer was telling a story to the butcher's second string. As he neared the end his shoulders began to shake. "Bring me another woman!" he shouted above his own laughter. "*This one's dead!*"

Mr. Scales swallowed a mouthful of beer the wrong way and choked. He staggered to his feet and made for the door. As he went, he noticed that although Miss Dogtinder had her back to him, she was watching in the mirror of a large, old-fashioned compact. He met her eye. It was bland, fishy, malignant. He clawed at the door and stumbled out into the dark Mews. He leant against the wall and held a hand over his heart.

Two powerful headlights swung into the cul-de-sac. Then the car stopped, reversed. The headlight swept over the wasteland. Mr. Scales saw Senator raise his head and for a second his eyes gleam red. The car stopped on the corner. A man got out of it and turned off the lights. He began to walk down Wharf Mews. As he passed the lantern on Alistair Starke's porch, Mr. Scales saw that it was George Heap. He was in evening clothes and he was smoking a cigar.

Mr. Scales was immediately reassured. He admired Sukie's uncle enormously. Physically, sartorially, morally, he was, in Mr. Scales's opinion, a proud survival of better days. *I been bein' daft*, thought the undertaker. *No need to get jumpy. Nobody's after you. I been workin' too 'ard, that's all. These quick thaws brings 'em down in droves.* He breathed a sigh of relief. He looked back at George Heap, warm with gratitude that his hero had dispelled the fears.

George Heap brushed a flake of ash off his impeccable lapel and crossed the Mews. Drawing off his gloves, he picked up a stone and hurled it at Senator.

# CHAPTER 14

HUGH took off his tie and hung it over the back of a chair. "Sukie," he said casually, "do you often cut up wood?"

They were in the kitchen. The washing-up was finished and Sukie was making Horlicks to take up to bed. Delighted that Hugh had broken the long silence, she was caught off guard. "No," she said. "Hardly ever because I nearly always miss. Why?"

Hugh caught her by the shoulders and glared down at her. "Then how do you account," he snapped, "for the fact that you struck both of your victims only once and in each case unerringly on the back of the skull?"

There was a short pause. Sukie's smile faded. "You pig!" she said hotly. "You were deliberately trying to trick me!"

"Are you asking the jury to believe that they stood there while you swiped at them, missed them, hacked at them again and again?"

Sukie tried to get away from him. Hugh held on to her. "There isn't any jury," she said, struggling.

"Don't stall."

"Don't you shout at me!"

"Answer me."

"I will not. I want my lawyer."

"*I* am your lawyer." He shook her. "You've been lying again."

The Horlicks boiled over. Sukie lost her temper. "Well, what do you expect?" she shouted. "I tell you one lot and you don't believe me, so I tell you the opposite and that's wrong too! *Whatever* I say is wrong! I'm fed up with being cross-examined."

Hugh let her go. He made the gesture of a barrister mutely appealing to the jury to appreciate the appalling difficulties of his case. He then leant against the splintered door and folded his arms. "You're not going to leave this room until you tell me the truth," he said distinctly.

Sukie looked at him. She knew immediately that this was no idle threat. He was wearing the expression which she privately called Battle of Jutland. She turned her back on him and began to arrange fruit on a plate. She knew that he was watching her. She sat down suddenly on a wooden chair. "All right," she said. "I don't know. Honestly, I'm all muddled up."

Half an hour later she had told him the whole story. Hugh had caught her out in only two minor lies. He was at last satisfied that this time he had got at the truth, that she genuinely remembered nothing about either murder. He also realized that, owing perhaps partly to his own attitude, she was almost convinced that she had committed both.

"You know what Heaps *are*," she said sadly. "They do forget things. Look at Granny. *She* didn't remember."

"Why did you confess?"

"Well, Mummy said ..."

"Victoria is ... not altogether responsible."

"Yes, she is," said Sukie, instantly aggressive. "So was Granny. She was hanged, wasn't she?"

Hugh took the tray of fruit and Horlicks from her and went out of the room. She followed him upstairs into the bedroom. He put the tray on the bedside table, lit the gas fire, and undid the zipper on the back of Sukie's dress.

"Don't worry, love," he said with more assurance than he felt. "We'll work out something." *Will we have to leave the country? Oh God, not Australia!*

Sukie was pulling her dress over her head. "I'm not worrying," she said from inside its folds. "I shall never be arrested."

Hugh sat down and took off his shoes. "What do you mean?"

Sukie threw the dress over a chair. "There won't be any witnesses," she said. She began to peel off her stockings. "Everybody is an accessory. None of them want to go to jug for ten years." She smiled reassuringly at Hugh. "I've got a plan," she added.

Hugh's heart sank. He dreaded his wife's little plots. Most of them had a certain cunning, but they were based upon some profoundly false assumption. He did not want to hear this one. He knew that it would only confuse him. Gloomily, he took off his socks.

Sukie wriggled into her nightdress and sprang into bed. She wrapped herself in a blue shawl, bit into an apple, and produced from beneath the pillows a bundle of large manila envelopes. She selected one of these and handed it to Hugh with unconcealed pride. He took it unwillingly. It was addressed to Mr. Tooley in red ink and capital letters.

"Now look here, Sukie ..."

"Open it."

Hugh opened it. It confirmed his fears immediately. A scruffy piece of paper lay in his hand. On it was written: *He went on and on. I had to put him down in the end. Aren't I awful? I'm always doing it. T. Tooley.* It smelt faintly of gin. Hugh flicked it impatiently. "What's this meant to be? Absolutely idiotic! It'd be hooted out of Court."

Sukie began to peel a tangerine. "Maybe," she said calmly. "But it helps to confuse the Prosecution." She pushed a piece of notepaper into his hand. "It incriminates."

Hugh glanced down at the notepaper. It was headed CASE AGAINST THOMAS TOOLEY. He groaned.

"Read it," said Sukie.

"Really, love, I know you mean well but ..."

"Read it."

Hugh read it reluctantly. *This witness, if not principal, is accessory after both facts. Discovered both A and B, made no attempt to inform police. Why? Eight times in Homes for Alcoholics, twice discharged as incurable. Note To Defending Counsel: Question this witness about animal on back of neck. This will make the jury laugh and be happy.*

Hugh threw it on to the bed. "No, honestly, Sukie. It simply won't do."

His wife took no notice. She handed him another envelope. Hugh made a determined effort not to look at it. He laid it down on the chest of drawers and took off his jacket. Out of the corner of his eye he read MISS DOGTINDER. He glanced at Sukie. She was eating grapes and writing in her notebook. He could not resist it; he picked up the envelope and opened it. Tied to a label was the sachet. On the label was written: *Exhibit found on scene of Crime B*. Hugh frowned at the elaborate alibi, the page of comments. The latter read: *Accessory after fact Two. Saw body being removed by two unauthorized people, did not inform police. Why? Questioning will reveal that this was because she saw a wild lion. A likely story! Tip to D.C.: weird, thinks she is Moon Prophet, etc. Prophesied earthquake Wales 1940. Where is it? Ridicule this witness. Bog the jury down.*

Hugh did not look at his wife. It occurred to him that if she were controlled she might make an excellent shyster. He took off his shirt. "That's all very well," he began. "But ..."

"Wait," said Sukie. "You've got to see them all. Then you get the panorama." She kicked under the bedclothes at an envelope lying on her feet.

Hugh picked it up. It concerned the Great Tabora. It contained a statement that Tabora had bought one axe in Smyrna, one in Croydon. "My God!" said Hugh. "How did you get this?"

Sukie held up a hand for silence. She took the page of notes out of his hand and read aloud, " 'Extremely suspect. Accessory after both facts. Buried A, slunk about with B (call Dogtinder, Beecher, you).' "

"Who?"

"You. 'Can witness explain signed affidavit about axes to your satisfaction? (Call me) Make the jury distrust him.' "

Against his will, Hugh was becoming interested. "He's a drunk," he said, "but I don't believe he's a killer."

"The Judge won't like him. He looks like one."

"Killer?"

"Judge."

Hugh sat down on the bed and picked up the dossier on Miles Tate-Grahame. It contained the broken test tube. He clicked his tongue impatiently and threw it into the wastepaper basket. Sukie watched it. From her expression Hugh knew that as soon as he turned his back she would fetch it and return it to the envelope. He turned to the notes. *Urgent*, he read. *Witness does not know much, therefore may be dangerous. Counsel: establish fact immediately that witness once won sizeable football pool. Prejudice jury against him with envy. Hints: Once invented dog-queller – turned down by Animal Society of which Victim A was member. Trying to invent hair dye, made guinea pigs go bald – more trouble. Blackmailer. Has extorted six pairs of socks (call myself). Has repulsive smile. Make him use it.*

Hugh blinked. He looked at his wife. She was kneeling in front of the dressing table cold-creaming her face. She met his eyes in the mirror and beamed. "Nearly forgot," she said, "what with everything."

Hugh stuffed the data on Miles back into its envelope and shook the case against Mrs. Filby on to the eiderdown. A small sepia photograph fluttered to the floor. Hugh picked it up. It showed Mrs. Filby and Mr. Bentley standing by a motor-bicycle combination. Sitting in the sidecar was an enormous cat. It had moved during the exposure and its head was an ectoplasmic blur.

"Where did you get this?"

"Beecher got it."

"That's burglary."

"Housebreaking. He got it in the afternoon."

Hugh sighed. Sukie scrubbed her face with a tissue, came over and sat down on the bed beside him. She handed him the page of notes and read it with him over his shoulder. *Instruction to Counsel: Witness is on our side. Challenge any teetotal member of jury with* propter affectum. *Make them like her. Memo to Me: find out why Bentley visited her every six months. Leave no stone unturned. Remember to tell Beecher to take Roarer to shady taxidermist for de-stuffing. Post skin under plain cover to Uncle George.*

Hugh did not comment. For a moment he wondered whether his wife's activities might not so confuse and amaze a Court of Law that she would get away with it. Her notes, handled by an expert counsel would acquire extraordinary significance. He scratched his head and took up the envelope marked MR SCALES. Inside was a warning that the man knew little or nothing about either murder, would probably tell the truth, and therefore must be questioned with the greatest of delicacy. This was followed by two questions. *Why would witness not sign my harmless statement? Why is Senator so neurotic?*

"Nothing there," said Hugh. "We can count him out."

"No we can't. Why isn't Senator happy?"

"What's that got to do with it?"

"It has."

"It would be more effective if you concentrated on one of them."

"Which? Miles?"

"All right." He looked at her curiously. "Why are you so dead against Miles?"

"His teeth." She passed him the last envelope.

Hugh opened it. It concerned Alistair Starke. Inside were the scrap of corduroy, the signed statement, and some cake crumbs. Hugh poked the latter gingerly.

"What are these?"

Sukie peered over his shoulder. "They're me," she said apologetically. "I was having a snack. Ignore them."

Hugh turned over the page of notes. *Hint to be dropped anonymously in Prosecution Chambers: witness is unreliable, blackmailer, accessory after both facts, had body on 19th inst Warning to Defense Counsel: He knows too much. Beware. If he chatters, encourage. Let him talk his head off; then call Beecher, Mrs. Filby, Me. We will corroborate us and prove he is liar.*

"Perjury," said Hugh.

"I know. It can't be helped."

Hugh tossed the notes on to the bed. "What about Beecher?" he asked.

"Beecher doesn't kill people."

"Me?"

"You're eliminated."

"Thanks. Mrs. Pickett?"

"She's out. She can't move fast. Something to do with her inside."

"Uncle George?"

"Don't be silly! He can't even look at gravy."

Hugh put on his pajamas and combed his hair. He watched his wife in the mirror. She was eating a pear and busily sorting out statements, notes, and clues. "I believe you're quite enjoying yourself," he said.

Sukie replaced the dossiers under her pillow. She looked up, considering. "Yes," she said thoughtfully. "I think I am. I suppose it's in the blood."

# CHAPTER 15

ALISTAIR STARKE, pacing his dirty hall, stopped and looked at himself in the mirror on the wall. "You are a bloody coward," he told his dishevelled reflection. He pointed a shaking finger at the haggard face. "*Do something!*" he roared. He sat down on a broken stool and tugged at his beard.

All day long, Marigold Tossit had lain in the cupboard under the stairs. All day long, Alistair had promised himself that as soon as it was dark he would take her out of his house and throw her away on the bomb site. Now night had fallen. He looked restlessly out of the window. He could just see the gaunt trees tossing on the wasteland. The storm would return soon. The thunder was grumbling over Chiswick.

Sukie, Hugh, Mrs. Filby, and Mr. Tooley had taken two bodies and a stolen lion in their stride. But Alistair, who was to a certain extent blackmailing all four of them, sat staring out of his grimy window, kicking his heels and shivering with panic. *I tell you that I can't do it by myself,* he informed his reflection. *You can and you know it ... I can't ... Oh, get a move on! ... I tell you that I need help ... Why? You've done all right so far ... They had help, didn't they? You need somebody to talk to ... Very well, yell for help. Coward! ... I'm going to ... I should ... Oh, shut up!* He snatched at the telephone and dialed the Lupus Street number. "Now look here!" he blustered immediately the receiver was removed at the other end of the line.

"Where?" inquired a voice with a slight lisp. "How can I look there, you silly boy?"

"Who are you? I want Beecher."

"Why?" asked the Queue irritably. "Always *Beecher*. And you can't speak to him either. He's out."

Alistair was about to slam down the receiver when it occurred to him that anybody connected with Beecher was almost certain to be a criminal. He decided to take a chance. "I'm in a jam," he muttered. "I need help."

There was a brief pause. "Oh," said the Queue. His tone had hardened.

109

"Come off it, conker! What have you got inside your helmet? Sand-wiches?"

"I'm not a policeman," said Alistair desperately. He mopped his fore-head. "Honestly, I'm not. I'm an artist. I ... I've got a beard. I'm an ac-complice of Mrs. Chandor's."

"Prove it," said the Queue.

Five minutes later, Alistair had persuaded him that he was neither a policeman, nor an informer, nor a member of a rival organization, and the Queue had agreed to come around and talk things over.

Beecher, who had been dispatched by Sukie Chandor to fetch Mari-gold, arrived at Alistair's front door in time to overhear most of this con-versation. He mauled the door-knocker and swore. He disliked Alistair and wanted him to suffer. He had protested bitterly against Sukie's or-ders. It had caused him considerable inconvenience to get Marigold into the artist's house and he considered that she should stay there until the man had been punished a great deal more. The fact that Alistair had sum-moned the Queue, particularly the Queue, infuriated him. The Queue was supposed to stay at home that night, alibiing Lights and Solly while they beat up a certain chemist off Frith Street. Beecher peered cautiously through the glass panel in the front door. Alistair was smiling now, look-ing at himself in the mirror and combing his hair.

Beecher bit the back of his hand. *I'll make you smile th' other side o' yer silly face!* he thought. He resisted the impulse to rush into the hall and hurt Alistair. Stepping off the porch, he trod on to the tiny lawn and stomped all over the flower bed. *I'll fix 'im*, he thought savagely. *Standin' there grinnin'*. He forgot his orders without a qualm. Alistair, he decided, should keep Marigold for at least another night. The Queue must be intercepted.

The only difficulty about this plan was that Beecher never knew where or at what level his lieutenant would enter a house. The Queue rarely used the same method twice. He might use the front door, approach on the flank, scale the back, or appear as if by magic on the roof. In theory and by prearrangement, Beecher could be in two places at once; in prac-tice, there were occasions when he needed an ally. This was one of them.

He took off his horrible cap and sucked thoughtfully at the cloth but-ton on its crown. He peered at his turnip watch. Solly and Lights were busy. Finger was in hospital. The Smiler was away for the weekend. Guts was Inside. Suddenly Beecher clapped his cap over his face. He stumbled out into the mews, rolling with suppressed laughter. *I got it!* he thought. *Albert Chivvers! I'll give ole Albert a treat!*

He stole down the Mews and slipped into the dark alleyway beside the Carp. He broke in through the larder window. He did not bother to use the silent saw on the wire mesh, but stood on the sill and kicked his way in. Lowering himself on to the floor, he trod into a basket of apples. The sensation pleased him. Standing in the basket, he broke a large piece off a fruit cake. He crammed it into his mouth, went through into the kitchen, and put the kettle on to boil. Munching, he went along the passage to the telephone. At the foot of the stairs, he met Mrs. Filby. She was wearing a quilted dressing gown, curlers, and she was clutching a poker. When she saw Beecher, she went red with rage.

Beecher took no notice of her. He inserted two annas in the telephone and dialed the number of the local police station. He pressed Button A and asked to speak to Constable Chivvers. Mrs. Filby dropped the poker.

" 'Ullo, tosh," growled Beecher. "Want to do yerself a drop o' good? Pop on yer galoshes an' 'op along to Wharf Mews." He replaced the receiver.

As he put it down, Mrs. Filby heard the small voice from the Station shouting down the wire. Dazed, she ran into the bar and examined the cash register. It was untouched. She heard Beecher stumping down the passage, turned and scuttled after him. *'E's after the 'am!* she thought. *'E'll swipe the radio! 'E'll knock off my checkbook!* She burst into the kitchen. Beecher was making a pot of tea.

The tumblers threw themselves off the stage and were succeeded by a performing dog and a man in ill-fitting jodhpurs. The dog was wearing a minute bowler hat. It was billed as The Dog Who Knows Too Much.

Tribling's little hands rustled in his box of chocolates. He popped a coffee cream into his mouth. He did not bite it, but left it lying on his tongue, prepared for a happy half-hour while it dissolved. "I can't see," he mumbled fretfully, "I can't see a thing."

George Heap glanced at his watch. He had intended Tribling to hate the seats. "Very well," he said smoothly. "Let us transfer." It was nine minutes ahead of schedule but the performing dog was more than he could bear. The creature was now answering questions, one bark for yes, two for no.

Tribling, who had dined far too well, refused to leave. He stood up and asked the dog's opinion on his iron shares. The dog ignored him. Tribling fell back onto his seat, helpless with laughter. The woman in the next seat smacked him on the knee. "You *are*!" she choked. George Heap glanced at her. She had a fat, vicious face. She would make a redoubtable witness.

The dog turned a rapid somersault, boxed with a monkey, fired a cannon, bowed itself off the stage. Red electric bulbs spelt the word Interval.

George Heap took Tribling firmly by the elbow. "Come," he said, "we will take a breath of air."

The Queue sprang off the bus at Tite Street. He made a wide detour and approached Alistair Starke's house from the northeast. Vaulting over Miles Tate-Grahame's wall, he crossed Alistair's back yard and entered gracefully through the kitchen window.

Albert Chivvers got off his bicycle outside the Chandors' house and chained the machine to a tree. *Wild goose chase*, he thought. *Some comic. Routine, routine, routine.* Clutching his truncheon, he walked as quietly as his boots would allow down the darker side of Wharf Mews. Forcing his way through the wooden palings on to the bomb site, he wondered what he was supposed to watch. He chose a tangle of brambles about halfway down, crouched behind it, and prepared to wait in ambush almost indefinitely.

In the passage which led to the foyer, Tribling was distracted by a large photograph of an old-fashioned beauty in sequin tights. "Those were the days," he remarked, staggering slightly. "The ta-ra-ra-boompsi days!"

George Heap controlled an urge to strangle the man at once. He took him by the elbow and steered him through an emergency exit. Tribling followed obediently, humming to himself. Their footsteps rang on the stone staircase. At the bottom, George Heap shot a quick glance down the dark cul-de-sac. There were no street lamps. At the end was the brightly lit main road. A bus passed, a taxi, two more buses. The Buick was parked ten yards away in a pool of deeper shadow.

"Come," said George Heap evenly. "A little spin to blow the cobwebs away."

"No," said the Queue, looking at Marigold with disapproval. "I don't do corpses. Whatever next!"

Alistair turned away to hide his mounting panic. "All right," he said with an effort at nonchalance. "No removal, no portrait."

The portrait had been the Queue's idea. The police photographers had inhibited him; it was always the full face and the profile. He badly wanted a three-quarter view painted in oils. He hesitated. "Well," he said. "Paint me first and then we'll see."

Silently, Alistair led the way to the studio.

Albert, cramped behind the brambles, wondered unhappily when dew began. He was about to shift his legs into a more comfortable position when he saw a flicker of light from inside the Carp. *Ho ho!* he thought.

He stood up, forced his way through the undergrowth, and slipped into the mews. His boots creaked on the cobbles. He stood under the window of the saloon bar listening. He had a moment of doubt. How many of them were there? Were they armed? Would they, as had happened recently to one of his colleagues, truss him up and leave him writhing on the wrong beat? *This 'ere's your big chance, Chivvers*, he thought. *Don't want to go off 'alf-cocked.*

He crawled along under the windows to the large garage next door. This would be the ideal place from which to watch and, if circumstances permitted, to attack. It took him some time, working busily with a nail file to unscrew the lock. This done, he edged himself inside, took off his helmet, and sat down on one of Senator's hoofs. The horse had been lying down. He lumbered up with a whinny of fear and began to trot around his stable.

"Sssss-ssh!" hissed Albert. "Stow it, will you?" But Senator had been badly frightened. He continued to run about, kicking up his heels and banging into the wooden partitions. Albert, with considerable courage, reached out in the darkness. He caught the animal by the mane and held on. Senator dragged him across the stable, turning his head to bite. Albert heard the click of the great square teeth and let go hastily. Resisting the impulse to hit Senator between the eyes with his truncheon, he retreated. He pushed the door to behind him and, cursing, hurried back to his lair on the bomb site.

Senator lay down and, in doing so, pushed open the door of his stable. He smelt the dark wind and immediately rose again. Never having been abroad at night before, he stood for a moment looking about him curiously. Then he tossed his head and advanced nervously into the mews, his hoofs clattering on the cobbles.

The Queue stood up on the model throne and scratched himself voluptuously. He had insisted upon being painted in a sarong. But at the same time he had refused to undress. He came over and stood behind Alistair's shoulder looking critically at the canvas. "That won't do," he said petulantly. "Make me more *brown*."

George Heap backed the car into a ruined arch. The traffic in King's Road was a faint rumble. The wind had dropped. The wasteland lay in grim silence. He switched off the headlights.

"We shall take a little stroll," he announced. "It will sober you up."

Tribling dropped his box of chocolates. "Don't want to sober up," he said peevishly. "On the tiles." He drank again from the flask which his host had provided.

George Heap took the scarf out of his pocket and tied it into a Magnus Hitch. His palms began to tingle. He knew again the feeling of extraordinary power and lucidity. He glanced around him. There was nobody in sight. He moved his feet inside his shoes, caressed the scarf, enlarged the noose.

"Good gracious!" said Tribling. "Look! A horse!"

Mr. Scales woke abruptly. He had dreamed that he heard a horse galloping under his window. The dream had been so vivid that he was vaguely disturbed. He got out of bed, threw open the window, and peered down at the stable door. It was open. He snatched his overcoat, fumbled into his boots, and stumbled, swearing, downstairs after Senator.

Outside, he stood still, straining his ears. In the cold, frosty air, sounds carried with uncanny clarity. Almost immediately he heard his horse cropping at the grass among the ruins. He wriggled through the broken palings and peered into the darkness. He could see nothing except the vague outlines of the shattered buildings. Uncertainly, he forced his way through a bush.

"Look where you're goin'!" snapped Albert Chivvers in a furious whisper.

Mr. Scales jumped. " 'Oo's that?" he asked hoarsely.

"Oh, go away," snarled Albert.

"Constable Chivvers!" Mr. Scales' relief was so great that he spoke vehemently. "*Vox faucibus haesit!*"

"That's right!" said Albert bitterly. "Shout! I don't care. 'Aven't you got any fireworks?"

"Fine brute," said Tribling doubtfully. "Close coupled."

George Heap ground his teeth. The horse was standing only a few feet away. It was just visible against the dark sky. It stood immobile, ominous, infinitely sinister. The Strangler shivered. He was reminded suddenly of an afternoon long ago, of the ethereal Hannah lying in a hammock, pointing a fan at him. "Never trust an animal," said her soft, light voice across the years. "They are creatures of darkness." George Heap wondered whether anyone had ever strangled a horse. The thought steadied him. He pulled on his gloves and turned to Tribling.

A man came running around the corner. It was Mr. Scales. Panting, he rushed up to Senator and grabbed him by the ear. He peered into the car, saw George Heap, and stiffened. Since he had seen the man bombarding Senator with stones, he no longer admired him.

"What d'you think *you're* doin'?" he said coldly. "Lucky for you 'e didn't kick your bus. Wouldn't of blamed 'im, neither." He pulled the horse away. "Come on, old man." A few yards away, George Heap heard him say in a breathless undertone, "You do that again, I'll turn you fur side inside, you 'ear!"

A light went on in Miles Tate-Grahame's house. The inventor appeared at the window. "Will you please be quiet!" he shouted. "What's going *on* out there?"

Forty feet away in the brambles, Albert Chivvers clawed at his face. He stood up and hurled his helmet into a ruined cellar. "Go *'ome!*" he screamed. " 'Ooever you are, go *'ome!*"

## CHAPTER 16

IT was after midnight when the first stealthy knock came on the Chandors' back door. Sukie, dressed for action in slacks and sweater, ran downstairs. She was worried. Something had obviously gone wrong. She had been expecting Beecher and Marigold since half past ten, her uncle since eleven. In the darkness she pressed herself against the back door waiting for the password upon which she had insisted.

"Who's there?"

"Boots, boots, boots," growled a resentful voice.

Sukie opened the door. Beecher pushed past her and kicked it shut. He was breathing heavily and grumbling under his breath. He staggered along the passage into the hall. Sukie followed him, lit a candle, and stood it on the table. "You're late," she said. "What happened?" Then she turned round and saw that Beecher was carrying Roarer. She seized his arm and shook it. "Where's Marigold?" she demanded.

Hugh appeared at the top of the stairs in dressing-gown and pajamas. He saw Roarer and hit himself in the forehead. "No!" he said loudly. "No. I damn well won't have it! Take it away!"

Sukie stamped her foot. "*Where's Marigold?*"

"I refuse to have that lion in my house!" roared Hugh. He started downstairs. "Take it away immediately."

Beecher stood the lion on the floor and leant against it. "You know what's good for you," he said hoarsely, "you'll get rid o' this brute *ec*

115

*dum*. It is a witness an' a clue an' an accessory. It's *'ot!* Chivvers finds it, you've 'ad it. An' Chivvers is outside in the scrub gettin' imself a suntan."

"*What?* Why? Somebody's ratted."

"Where's Marigold?" insisted Sukie. "Why did you bring *him*? I wanted *her*."

"Mrs. Filby said to say as she's given 'im notice. She won't 'ave 'im not another minute, she says."

There was a tinkle of breaking glass from the kitchen, the squeak of a finger dragged down a pane. A voice said angrily, "Oh fork!"

Beecher and Hugh simultaneously leaped at Roarer. Hugh grabbed the head, Beecher the tail. They tried to push him into the dining room but he got stuck halfway. Hugh vaulted over his back through the doorway and began to pull.

"Push, you fool!" he ordered desperately.

"Push yerself," said Beecher.

"Back. Tuck the tail in."

"Tail's stiff."

"For God's sake!"

"Won't bend."

"*Break* it off!"

"*Well!*" said the Queue from the far end of the passage. "Well *really!*"

Beecher straightened up with a horrible scowl. Hugh peered over Roarer. Sukie sat down abruptly on the stairs. The Queue had Marigold over his shoulder in a fireman's grip.

"Who are you?" snapped Hugh. "Who *is* that man?"

The Queue put Marigold carefully into a chair. "Compliments of Mr. Starke," he said. "Prezzy."

"Who *are* you?" shouted Hugh.

"Leave him alone," said Sukie. "He's on our side."

The back doorbell rang, and rang again. For a moment nobody moved. The burglars reacted first. Beecher snatched Marigold and ran upstairs. The Queue threw open the cupboard under the stairs, pushed the Hoover roughly aside, and leapt back to Roarer. Hugh sprang to help him. They seized the lion and bundled him into the cupboard. Hugh started upstairs after Beecher. The Queue faded into the dining room. The bell rang insistently. Sukie shot a distracted glance round the hall. The carpet was rucked up, but otherwise it looked quite normal. She ran to the back door.

It was Miss Dogtinder. She wore a woolen dressing gown and a blue chenille hair net. She darted into the kitchen, slammed the door, and leant against it. "Sanctuary!" she panted. "The lion is back!"

"There has been no lion here," shouted Hugh from halfway upstairs. "No lion whatever."

Miss Dogtinder wrung her hands. "My goat! Mr. Chandor! If anything happens to Joan ..." She scuttled along the passage with Sukie at her heels.

When they reached the hall, Hugh had disappeared. Miss Dogtinder flung open the dining-room door. The Queue was sitting on the table nibbling a biscuit.

"Who are you?" demanded the herbalist.

"M.Y.O.B.," said the Queue coldly.

There was a thud overhead. Miss Dogtinder jumped. She clutched her dressing gown around her and started upstairs. "Mr. Chandor!" she cried.

"Stop her!" said the Queue.

"It doesn't matter," said Sukie. "She knows. It's just the lion she mustn't see." She took a biscuit out of the tin. "It's tricky, isn't it? They all know different bits. You have to remember it all."

Beecher climbed in through the window. "Drain pipe wants mendin'," he grumbled. " 'S'broke. Very dangerous." He rubbed his hands on the seat of his trousers. "I put the young lady in the linen cupboard. 'Oo was creatin'?"

"Miss Dogtinder."

"You know what *I* think?" said the Queue. "I think that woman is a *man*."

Sukie leant out of the window. "What's Albert *doing* out there?" she asked moodily.

" 'E needs a rest," said Beecher. "A nice rest in a splint."

"You're a monster," said the Queue. "Why don't you stick to nicking turkeys?" Beecher advanced upon him. The Queue stood up hurriedly. "I say what I think," he said, sticking out his chin. "Always have, always shall."

Beecher walked around him in a half circle. "Want yer arm snatched off?" he inquired.

The front doorbell rang. Sukie hesitated then ran into the hall. Hugh's head appeared over the banisters at the top of the stairs. Sukie went to the door.

"Who's there?" she whispered.

"Stop this nonsense immediately!" said George Heap angrily from outside. "Open the door before I lose my temper."

Sukie let him in. He had cigar ash on his normally immaculate lapels and his face was dark with rage. He drummed his cane impatiently on the tiled floor.

"The trunk is in the car," he snapped. "Fetch it. Insert the body. Replace it." Beecher came out of the dining room. "Who is this individual?"

"That," said Hugh bitterly from the top of the stairs, "is one of my wife's new friends."

"Kindly fetch my trunk."

Beecher pursed his lips. " 'Oo? Me?"

George Heap's eyes flashed. "Yes. You."

"Please," said Sukie quickly.

Beecher went out of the front door and slammed it behind him.

George Heap turned on his niece. "Come," he said, clicking his fingers irritably. "The body."

"It's terribly nice of you," said Sukie. "Will you take the lion too?"

George Heap made a valiant effort to control himself. But on top of his bitter disappointment about Tribling, this was too much. He closed his eyes and hit the banisters with his cane. "Must I," he shouted, "bear the entire burden of your crass bungling? Do you imagine that I have nothing better to do than fetch and carry your victims? You have an army of accomplices. Why has this body not disappeared in a civilized and clueless manner? Why has this lion not been presented to a museum? *Why is the wasteland infested with your mad cronies?*"

Beecher reappeared with a large wardrobe trunk. It was plastered with the labels of fashionable hotels from Calcutta to California. Beecher dropped it with a thud on George Heap's foot. The Strangler did not appear to notice it. Beecher looked at him curiously. Hugh started downstairs with Marigold. Miss Dogtinder was behind him. She saw George Heap, clutched at the neck of her dressing gown, screamed, and rushed back into the drawing room. George Heap snatched the gardenia from his buttonhole and threw it on the floor. The Queue came out of the dining room eating an apple.

"Who are *you*?" demanded the Strangler.

"Madame Prunier," said the Queue huffily. "Don't you shout at me!"

The front doorbell rang.

Hugh, halfway downstairs, turned and rushed back upwards. Beecher leapt after him. The Queue darted into the dining room. George Heap and Sukie were left standing in the hall. The bell rang again, a loud authoritative peal. George Heap prodded his niece with the cane.

"Answer it," he said. His face twitched. "No doubt it is another of your corybantic allies."

It was Albert, slightly out of breath. "What's goin' on 'ere?" he asked. "I 'eard a scream. Anythin' wrong?"

"No, no," said Sukie quickly. "Not a thing."

"Was a scream."

"Yes. The um radio. Play. Very exciting."

Albert looked up and down the road. "Somethin' goin' on 'ere tonight."

Sukie opened her eyes wide. "Oh? What?"

Albert looked dissatisfied. "Dunno," he admitted. "I 'ad a tip. Somethink's goin' to 'appen. People all over the shop. Why don't they go to bed? I don't like it." He grinned suddenly, clasping his hands behind him and bending his knees, caricaturing himself. "My suspicions is aroused," he said ponderously. "Not jokin' though, you see anythin' untoward, you just 'oller. I'll be right outside."

"No, really," said Sukie earnestly. "There's absolutely no need for that. Everything's fine."

Albert tapped himself on the helmet. "No troub," he said. "That's what I'm for." He nodded at the Buick. "Tell nunky to move on, will you? 'E can't park there." He saluted and marched away.

Sukie shut the door. Hugh appeared at the top of the stairs with Beecher behind him. The Queue slid out of the dining room. George Heap sat down on a chair.

"It's not *my* fault," said Sukie defensively. "What could I *do*?"

Half an hour later, George Heap had left empty-handed. Miss Dogtinder had been escorted home. Albert patrolled the road outside; and Sukie, Hugh, Beecher, and the Queue sat despondently in front of the drawing-room fire and, by the light of a candle, unpicked Roarer. He was stuffed with horsehair and kapok and there was a bar of steel inside his tail.

## CHAPTER 17

SUKIE woke first. She grabbed at Hugh. He sat up grumbling, shaking his head. His eyes focused slowly. "Oh yes!" he said. "Oh my God!" He leapt out of bed and rushed out of the room.

Sukie struggled into her clothes. There was somebody clattering about in the kitchen. She ran downstairs still pulling on her sweater. Hugh was on one knee just inside the front door, peering through the letter box.

"Has he gone?"

"I can't see him."

Sukie ran into the kitchen. There was a saucepan of coffee simmering on the stove and a bowl of shelled eggs on the table. The Queue came in through the back door. He was wearing an apron. He had a pair of nail scissors in one hand and a small bunch of herbs in the other.

"There's no china tea," he said accusingly.

Sukie pushed back her hair. "We always have coffee. What's the time?"

"Don't know."

"Where's Beecher?"

"Don't know."

"Where's Albert?"

"Don't know, don't care."

The front door bell rang. Sukie ran into the hall. Hugh was just disappearing around the bend of the stairs. Sukie did up the placket of her skirt and opened the door.

It was Mrs. Pickett. She sailed into the hall and immediately announced that she was on strike and did not intend to do a stroke. She looked disapprovingly at Sukie's ruffled hair and marched through into the kitchen. The Queue came out of the larder holding a pound of butter.

" 'Oo are you?" snapped Mrs. Pickett.

The Queue turned his back. "If one more person asks me that," he said, "I'll *scream*."

Mrs. Pickett peered into the coffee saucepan, turned up the gas, and watched it boil. The Queue clapped a hand over his eyes and moaned.

"Did you *see*?" He appealed to Sukie through his teeth. "Flagrant, quite *flagrant*."

Mrs. Pickett drew a breath for her morning bulletin. "Been a miscarriage o' justice," she remarked happily. "The 'Eavies 'ave locked up Bash Adams. Still tryin' to prove 'e's the Strangler. Bert says Bash wouldn't never do a thing like that, not outside the ring. Loiterin' with Intent! Bert says 'e 'ad Intent but was only Natural." She went on without a pause. "You see Miss Tossit? Went there 's'mornin' an see neither 'air nor 'ide. Asked Mr. Tabora an' e' turned on me somethin' wild. Well, I want me pay an' I says so. 'E says to collect from Miss Dogtinder 'oo is growin' 'ashish on Government property. Well, I dunno. *You* seen Miss Tossit?"

"Not today."

Mrs. Pickett picked up a fork and idly beat up the eggs in the basin.

The Queue screamed. "Oh! She *beat* them! *Beat*, I saw it!"

Mrs. Pickett dropped the fork. "What's eatin' *you*?" she asked aggressively.

"*Stir*," said the Queue. "*Stir*, you savage."

Sukie left them. She went upstairs. Hugh put his head around the bedroom door. He was pulling on his trousers.

"Who was that?" he whispered. "Who's screaming now?"

"Nothing. Where's Beecher?"

"I don't know. It's half past ten. Your uncle'll be here at eleven. I'm packing Marigold." The trunk was in the middle of the floor. Marigold was inside it. Hugh shut the lid. "We've got to get Roarer. Did you clean up the kapok?"

"Oh crumbs!" said Sukie. "Go and tell the Queue to stall Mrs. Pickett."

They ran downstairs together. Sukie ran into the dining room and saw that the kapok was going to be too much for her. "Bring the Hoover!" she shouted. She locked the door and began to collect the claws. Almost immediately there was a soft knock.

"Who?"

"Me."

Hugh came in wheeling the Hoover. "It's all right," he said. "They're making a cake."

Sukie was looking doubtfully from the kapok to the Hoover. "We'll never get it all in. We'll choke it."

Hugh looked at her. "Please," he said. "Not that word. Not *any* of those words. If you don't mind." He stared at the folded lion skin on the table. "Where's Beecher?"

"I don't know. *I* just asked *you*."

George Heap woke late and lay gazing at the ceiling. He had slept fitfully, his dreams dominated by closeups of Tribling's carotids.

During the Water Spectacle, he had been tempted to perform an impromptu trucidation on the way home. When, however, the two returned to the car at the end of the performance, Tribling had immediately fallen into a tipsy sleep. George Heap had tried several times to wake him before he accepted defeat. One could not kill a man asleep. It was not cricket. Anyway, he had set his heart upon the Wharf Mews wasteland. Perhaps this evening, after the disposal of his niece's victims, her hooligans would have vacated his chosen site. Perhaps this evening ...

He got out of bed, glanced at his watch, and saw that he was too late for breakfast. Biting his lip, he slid into his dressing gown, collected his bath towels, and stalked along the corridor to the bathroom. The door was locked.

"Won't be a minute," sang Tribling's voice from inside. He was reading again. George Heap distinctly heard him turn a page.

Miles Tate-Graham finished his breakfast and put his egg-smeared plate into the saline tank to soak. He then went over to the laboratory window where his shaving mirror hung and smeared his chin with a yellow paste, an invention of his own. He sat down on the window sill to wait until his beard dissolved.

From this vantage point, he saw Alistair Starke come to his bedroom window, still wearing pajamas, and train a pair of field glasses on to the Chandors' house. Miles turned curiously to see what the artist was looking at. Hugh and Sukie were apparently cleaning their dining room. Sukie had her hair tied up in a scarf and was plying a Hoover. Hugh was standing on a chair dusting the top of a cupboard. The air was full of what looked like flying feathers. Hugh suddenly saw Miles, leaped off the chair, and drew the curtains. Miles scowled. *Extraordinary*, he thought. *Absolutely unpredictable*. He picked up a spatula and began to scrape the paste and the rotted beard off his face.

The Great Tabora opened the parcel from his aunt in Australia, took out the pound of honey, and carried it into the garden to bury it. Miss Dogtinder was out there, milking Joan. She looked at Tabora and bowed distantly. The lion tamer knelt by the corner flower bed, removed the wedge of turf, and lowered the honey carefully into his cache. He had five pounds now. The first one, he gloated, must be nearly mature. He replaced the turf, stood up, and glanced puzzled at Miss Dogtinder. The herbalist had taken off one shoe and was peering at it. Joan was watching her sideways, eating a piece of newspaper. *Nuts*, thought Tabora. He put on his top hat and went back into his house.

Sukie straightened up and patted the Hoover. "It won't eat any more," she said. "Not even a handful. It's full."

Hugh went over to the window, parted the curtains, and leant his forehead against the cold panes. He stared out into the garden. The snow had almost disappeared but the semi-sphere of ice from the broken bird bowl still lay under the pear tree. Mrs. Pickett was standing on it, trying to break it, puffing at a cigarette, and scratching her head with a twig.

Just above the tree, an upper window was flung open in the Carp. Mr. Tooley leant out and blatantly threw two bottles into Mr. Scales's yard next door. He then brushed his hands together, shut the window, and disappeared. Hugh frowned. He saw suddenly that Miles Tate-Grahame was still watching him from the laboratory window. The inventor's mouth was open and he had a yellow paste over half his chin.

The phone rang. Sukie dropped the Hoover. She gave Hugh a startled look and ran into the hall.

"Yes?" she whispered.

"It is I," said George Heap tersely. "Ten minutes. Pack the grip. Leave the older of your stewards. Quit the house."

"I'll stay and help."

"You will not. I shall park the car before your house and spend ten minutes in the public house. During that time, your gorilla will place the grip in the boot. Is that understood?" He rang off.

The Queue put his head around the kitchen door. "Nobody's to open the oven," he said, and vanished.

Beecher came in at the front door.

"You picked the lock," said Sukie angrily. Beecher shuffled. "Where have you *been*?"

Beecher raised a cauliflower eyebrow. "Went to get the milk."

Mr. Scales ordered strong ale. He had no funeral scheduled so he would not drink his rum until 10:25 in the evening. He noticed that Mrs. Filby was wreathed in smiles. She hummed to herself as she poured his beer.

"Got the 'Ouse to meself again," she said happily. Then, "Oh. Pardon. Was forgettin' you didn't know."

"Didn't know *what*?" asked Mr. Scales tetchily.

Mrs. Filby wagged a finger at him and turned away with an ungainly little skip.

Sukie came in. She had small pieces of fluff in her hair and was looking anxious. She pushed thirty shillings across the counter. Mrs. Filby took the notes without a word. Alistair came out from the passage and held out his hand.

"No," said Sukie. "Hugh knows."

"Possibly," said Alistair, fluttering his fingers. "But at the moment some law-abiding characters might think that your house was over-tenanted."

Sukie glanced at her watch. "Oh, no, they wouldn't." She added nastily, "So you can jolly well creep back into your cheese."

For a moment Alistair was disconcerted. Then he turned on Mrs. Filby. "I will have a large gin-and-French," he said threateningly.

Mrs. Filby beamed. "*Oh* no, you won't!" she said triumphantly. "They've gone."

"*Where* have they gone? It, I mean."

Mr. Scales wanted to join in this conversation. "Some go up, some go down," he said tentatively.

"Down *where*?"

"Leapin' flames."

Alistair frowned. "I'm not trying to be difficult," he said impatiently, "but I don't understand you."

At the far end of the bar, Mr. Tooley perpetrated a monstrous belch. He did not apologize or even look up. He was arranging a row of ginger-ale bottles under the counter.

" 'Ere!" said Mrs. Filby loudly. "You tryin' to break the windows?"

Mr. Tooley grunted. He held up a glass of ginger ale. "Turned over new leaf," he mumbled.

" 'Bout time," said Mrs. Filby, dissatisfied.

"New leaf," said Mr. Tooley. He looked at his cache with satisfaction. Fourteen bottles; the mixture was one third whisky, one third Drambuie, one regrettable third ginger ale to provide the bubbles, and four melted cachous to each bottle. It had taken him nearly two hours to replace the caps, but never, in his opinion, had time been better spent.

Miles Tate-Grahame came in and hung up his mackintosh on the weighing machine. "Either," he remarked sourly, "the quality of your bitter has improved out of all recognition or this neighborhood has been taken over by gremlins. Last night ..."

"That's cheating," said Sukie hotly. "You got the socks."

"Socks," said Mr. Scales quietly to himself.

The butcher's second string came in with a notebook open in his hand. He approached Mr. Scales diffidently.

"Little sweep on the three o'clock," he said. "Bob."

Alistair and Sukie exchanged a glance.

"How does *he* ..."

"Sss-sh!"

"Did you ..."

"Shut up."

Mr. Scales looked at them suspiciously. He waved the butcher's second string away. "No," he said. "Whatever it is, I don't want it in the first place. I don't know what's goin' on in the second place and even if I did know what was goin' on in the first place, I wouldn't want it in the second place. 'Op it."

The butcher's second string approached Sukie. "Now I *know* you'll want to be in on this," he said leering.

"How do you know? You don't know a thing."

"I know one thing," snapped the beefy man, instantly aggressive. "You take that tone to me, you don't get *my* offal."

Alistair nudged Sukie. "Pass it off," he whispered out of the side of his mouth. "He's bluffing."

"You're nothing to do with the offals," said Sukie. "You only make the sausages."

"*Reely*?" said the butcher's second string unpleasantly. " 'Oo fetches

124

an' carries the *carcasses*, tell me that. Ar. Thought that would make you fink. 'Oo knows the good from the off? 'Oo knows which ones to get rid of quick an' which ones want 'angin'?"

Sukie swallowed. She did not look at Alistair. She could hear him breathing behind her shoulder. "Mr. Tabora will pay you," she said, sighing. "He owes it to Mr. Starke and Mr. Starke owes it back again to me."

"I do not," said Miles Tate-Grahame to nobody in particular, "believe in ghosts, fairies, or quaint little leprechauns. I am not prepared to believe that on three pints of postwar bitter I have hallucinations. There was ..."

Miss Dogtinder marched in. She looked at Miles's green pullover, closed her eyes, and sucked in her breath through her teeth. "Green!" she said. "*Green!* Today of all days. Oh you unfortunate man!" She bore down upon Alistair. "You owe me thirty shillings. You bought fifteen tickets from the Guild and deferred payment."

Alistair passed her the thirty tickets he had bought from the butcher. "Here," he said savagely. "Now please leave me alone. I haven't made a penny out of this."

Mr. Scales scratched his head. They were at it again. They were mad, all of them. Disturbed, he stared out of the window. There was a man on a ladder opposite pasting a new poster on to the hoarding on the bomb site. Humphrey Bogart pointed an automatic straight into the saloon bar. The gun had a flash of flame coming out of it. Mr. Scales turned away, leaning back out of the line of fire. He looked curiously at the mad drinkers. Sukie Chandor was whispering with Alistair Starke. A hand came around from the Ladies' Bar, Doris Pickett's voice said, "Saturday," Sukie, without interrupting her conversation, put into it thirty shillings, and it disappeared. Hugh Chandor came in. He went up to his wife and Mr. Scales distinctly heard him murmur, "They're coping now. The old boy's in a filthy temper. Are you giving anything to Tabora?" Sukie shook her head. "*He's* paying *me*," she said. Hugh frowned. "You may have to give it back," he said. "I think he saw. If he starts nattering about a trunk ..." His voice faded. Mr. Scales strained his ears but he could hear no more.

"Trunk," he said quietly to himself.

The Great Tabora arrived with his customary flourish. He drew a roll of notes out of his pocket and without a word handed two to Alistair. Sukie took them from Alistair and handed them to the butcher's second string. Mr. Tooley lurched over and peered into her glass. "What you drinkin'?" he demanded.

Sukie looked surprised. "Ginger ale."

"Well, *don't!*" barked Mr. Tooley. " 'Smine."

Beecher came in. He went over to Sukie and raised a thumb in an eloquent gesture. "Where's the Queue?" asked Sukie. "Gone 'ome," said Beecher. " 'E 'ad to do the laundry."

Alistair Starke was paying for his drink with two Weaver tickets. Mrs. Filby, grumbling, eventually accepted them and presented them as change to Miles Tate-Grahame. "What's the meaning of this?" said Miles indignantly. "Oh be quiet!" said Mrs. Filby. "Don't understand it meself. Barter, Mr. Starke says. Take it an' don't create."

"You're off, Tooley," said Mr. Tooley aloud. "Now you're off! There's a boy!"

"Where's Uncle George?" asked Sukie. Beecher jerked a thumb towards Humphrey Bogart. "Leave your problems until tomorrow," said Miss Dogtinder. "A disastrous day for all Sun-Cancerites! Disastrous! Absolutely *foul*." She plunged her hand into the neck of her blouse and brought forth a knitted shoulder strap.

They were all there, thought Mr. Scales. All of them. None of them what they seemed. All of them a little mad.

Hugh, standing by the bar, was thinking much the same. He, however, did not dismiss the problem as carelessly as Mr. Scales. *One of these apparently normal people*, he was thinking, is *more than eccentric. One of them has a rogue lion in his cellar. One of them, unless I'm right off the track, is a killer.* He looked involuntarily at Sukie. She looked up at him with wide green eyes and smiled faintly. Uneasily he took her hand. "There's something I can't quite remember," he said. "Something ..."

The door swung back and banged against the weighing machine. George Heap stalked in. The drinkers turned to stare at him. Mr. Scales half rose. A little of Miles Tate-Grahame's bitter slopped out of his glass. Miss Dogtinder turned away her head and blushed. Sukie started forward. In the sudden silence Doris Pickett's voice rang out in the Ladies' Bar.

"Bert likes 'em jugged, but I put my foot down."

"Larst time I done one," offered Mae, "Jim come into the kitchen an' *skid*. 'What's up?' 'e says. 'Been a murder?' "

"Chronic!" said Lil. "Drip, drip, drip all over the Inner Circle."

"Oh, the *blood!*"

"Runnin' like water."

"Blood, blood, blood!"

George Heap laid a hand over his eyes and swayed. He pushed Sukie and Miss Dogtinder roughly out of his way and tottered out into the passage.

He regained equilibrium at the top of the cellar stairs, throwing back his shoulders and blinking rapidly. The first thing he saw when he recovered sufficiently to glance around was Mossop. The cat lay halfway down the passage, watching him. Its eyes gleamed in the subaqueous beam from the skylight. Another damned animal who *knew!* George Heap turned away. Mossop streaked past him into the kitchen. The Strangler stared, amazed. The derelict old cat crouched at the ready, dangerous and mysterious. Its yellow eyes gave no hint of what it knew was about to happen. It watched indifferently as a pair of feet stole silently along the passage behind George Heap. It watched the feet stop, the weight go forward on to the toes. An arm was raised. George Heap turned. He threw up his hands but it was too late. He was struck a crushing blow over the medulla. He staggered. A push. He stumbled on the top stair, grabbed at the banister, missed, and disappeared headlong down the steep stairs to the cellar.

## CHAPTER 18

GEORGE HEAP picked himself up slowly. He was badly shaken and bruised. He was conscious of a swelling lump on the back of his head but he refrained from touching it. There might be ... the skin might be broken. One wrist, he discovered, was slightly sprained. He clenched his hand and a sharp pain shot up his arm. Gnawing his lip, he vowed that although this might handicap him, it would not prevent him strangling Tribling that evening. This thought calmed him. He stood up and adjusted his tie.

The darkness seemed almost solid. The Strangler had never before been in the cellar or even known of its existence. Presumably, he had been bundled through a trap door. Extraordinary. Somebody had hit him hard. Why? More important, who? Who had had the insolence to strike *him*? And particularly with that damned cat watching. The accursed animal had *known*. It had deliberately held his eyes while its confederate had struck from behind. The gardenia had fallen out of his buttonhole.

A throaty gurgle startled him. He moved towards it and found the rough, damp wood of a barrel. It occurred to him that he must in some way attract attention to his plight. He did not want to shout for help unless it were absolutely necessary. The thought of being rescued by a publican was repellent. He felt carefully over the barrel and found the rubber feed. He pulled, and a jet of beer sprayed his feet. He stepped back hastily. The mild spread after him. He splashed out of it. The smell sickened him. He stood listening. His feet were cold, his socks wet through. The beer was still rushing out of the barrel. He wondered how much there was of it. It had felt like a large barrel, probably about forty gallons. Again, it began to ooze around his feet. He frowned, clicking his tongue irritably, feeling his way along a dank wall. It stopped abruptly, forming a right angle. He tripped on the bottom stair.

Halfway up, his outstretched hand found something soft. He stopped and felt it cautiously. It was material. Rubbing it between his fingers, he diagnosed it as some sort of heavy fustian. Beneath it was something hard and rounded. He pinched this. With a sigh of exasperation, he realized that it was a human leg. Somebody was standing above him, trying to alarm him. It was undoubtedly his assailant, the coward who had struck him from behind. George Heap smoothed his mustache. *Very well*, he thought. He checked himself. It was hardly the psychological moment to kill a man when there was already a dead woman in the back of his car. Then again, there was Tribling scheduled for the evening. One must not exaggerate. A new thought struck him. He touched the material again, feeling more carefully. It was a skirt. His attacker had been a woman.

"Sukie," he said with asperity. "Open the door before I forget myself."

No answer. George Heap tapped a fingernail on his teeth. He knew a moment of uncertainty. If this were not his niece, it was either Mrs. Filby or Miss Dogtinder. In either case, he decided, he would put years on to her age. But he would not, unless it was absolutely imperative, kill her.

He took a handful of the skirt and drew it gently down the stairs. It followed him obediently. He could hear its wearer breathing. As he reached the bottom step, he trod, with a shiver of disgust, back into the beer. The smell was overpowering.

"Have you a light, Madam?" he asked politely. He intended by his very courtesy to create a weird impression.

A faint rattle, a hand feeling its way down his arm, a box of matches placed in his palm. George Heap bowed in the darkness, drew out a match, and scratched it against the box. He was looking down. The first thing he saw was the axe. It was new and gleaming with a bright yellow handle. For a sickening moment he wondered whether he were dead, reunited with his mother. He dropped the match. An axe! Photographically, he remembered the result of an axe combined with a loss of temper. He realized with anger that his hands were shaking. He moved away to review the situation. If the woman standing silently in the dark were his niece, it was unlikely that she would respond to reason. He remembered with a shudder himself in his little Norfolk suit clinging to his mother's skirts, running away, hiding in the shrubbery, calling desperately, "Mama, you *mustn't!* Not Beauchamps!"

Unable to endure these ghosts in the darkness, he fumbled for another match. The flame rose steadily. He saw that the fustian was not a skirt, but a cloak with a scarlet lining. He looked up and met the flat, determined gaze of the Great Tabora.

"Ah!" he said involuntarily. His immediate feeling was one of relief. The match burnt his fingers. He blew it out and lit another one. "May I inquire why you attempted to kill me?" he asked, frowning. "I presume that was your intention?"

Tabora nodded. He seemed preoccupied. He looked with distaste at the foaming tide, took off his cloak, and folded it over a barrel.

"Suppose," said George Heap sardonically, "that I were to scream?"

Tabora found Mr. Tooley's candle. George Heap proffered the match. The wick was wet. It spluttered. Tabora dropped hot wax on to a cask and set the candle upright in it.

"Help yourself," he said. "Doubt if anyone would hear you."

"To what," said George Heap tartly, "do I owe that cowardly assault?" He was affronted, but at the same time genuinely intrigued. He realized that for the first time in years, he had shaken off his ennui.

Tabora gave him a hard look. "Sure," he said. "But you spill first." His knuckles whitened on the handle of the axe. "How come my lion's in your rumble seat?"

George Heap sat down on an empty barrel and lifted his feet out of the beer. Beecher, he recalled, had dropped the lion skin in the road. "I have no need of it," he said coldly. "If you desire, the pelt shall be returned to you."

Tabora snorted impatiently. "Nuts," he said. "Don't give me that. You, friend, knew too much."

"*Knew*?" said George Heap, stung. "I really must protest against your use of the preterite."

"*How d'you get my lion?*"

"I understand that your first victim was buried in its place."

"Bentley?" Tabora stared. "Cheese!" he said. "How d'you like that! I looked all over."

The candle had drooped. George Heap straightened it. His hand was unsteady. This, then, was the man who had robbed him of his favorite victim. "Why, may I ask," he said harshly, "did you select poor old Bentley?"

"Poor old Bentley *nothing*!" said Tabora savagely. "That bird bled me dry. He was on to us from the first."

"Us? I'm afraid that I don't understand you."

"Who cares?" said Tabora. He wiped the blade of the axe on his sleeve. "Come on, come on. Turn around."

George Heap stood up. "My dear fellow, surely if you wish to enlist my cooperation, you must first gain my sympathy?" He tore his eyes away from Tabora's neck. He realized that he would probably be obliged to kill the man. "Kindly explain yourself."

Tabora considered this, balancing the axe in his hand.

"Won't you sit down?" asked George Heap.

Tabora hesitated, then sat down on a barrel the far side of the candle. "You ever see my act?" he asked.

George Heap shook his head.

Tabora ran a hand through his hair and scowled into the shadows. "Roarer weighed more than any other cat behind bars," he said heavily. After a slight pause, he added, "That's a lot of lion."

George Heap turned up his coat collar. The thought was unattractive. "I do not care for animals," he said.

"Roarer was O.K. at first. We were just like that." Tabora crossed his fingers. He was holding the axe with only one hand now. "You never know with cats," he said. "One spring, he acts up. Whams me in the shoulder. Well, that's nothing. One time or another they all try to pull something. But the next night he does it again. *So what?* I think. But then I think some more." He moved restively. "Roarer's put me up at the top of the bill. I've had some of the other and I don't like it. So what happens? I put another guy on the bars with a rod. I'm taking no chances. Next performance, they come in one by one – the panthers, the leopard, and the jaguar. Then there's a pause before Roarer breaks. He comes in that night low to the ground. He got a big hand as usual. Most nights he lets out a roar then. But that night he kept his big mouth shut. He just looked at me. And he looked *mean*. For the first time, I feel myself begin to sweat. In the ring that's bad. I wasn't putting my head in his mouth *that* night. I don't want a shave that close. Well, we got through that show but he played up all the way. Just *looking* at me." He flapped a hand impatiently. "Hell, *you* wouldn't know."

"Indeed I do," said George Heap warmly.

"Yair?" said Tabora scornfully. "Well, I know the answer to that one. I give him a shot of dope to quiet him down. Next day he comes into the ring like a lamb. And you know what? I lost my nerve." He snapped his fingers. "Just like that!"

George Heap lit a cigar. His sympathy was aroused. "Very understandable," he said. He was beginning to want to spare this man. He wondered whether, if he were to shout for help, anybody would hear and come to Tabora's rescue.

"Yep," said Tabora moodily. "One of those things. You lose your nerve after a plane crash. All right, you go up again. Maybe you get it back.

Cats are different. Lose your nerve with a cat and they never forget it. I tell you I got to *hate* that cat. It was him or me and we both knew it. And I had to play along because I knew that without him it meant back to the one-night stands. So I step up the dope. One night he drops off in the ring." Tabora dragged a hand over his face. "If there's anything that kills an act like that, it's the key cat yawning. So happened the Boss didn't see. But another guy did. Guess who."

George Heap was deeply interested. Forgetfully, he lowered his feet into the beer, then hastily withdrew them. "Bentley," he said.

"Right. That little snide spots it at once. He puts on the screws. He's a member of some Society. He's got me where he wants me. I pay up. But that's only the beginning. Couple of months later it's got so that he takes the big slice and I get the chicken feed. I'm in a spot. What would you have done?"

"My dear fellow." George Heap spread his hands and smiled diffidently.

Tabora glanced at him across the candle flame. "I'll tell you what *I* did," he said curtly. "One night I'm putting the panther through the hoops. Suddenly Roarer gives a goddam great yawn and jumps me. We both go down. The clunks outside think it's part of the act. The guy on the bars can't shoot – me and Roarer are all mixed up. Well, I think, this is It. Suddenly, he lays off. He's tired, bored, I don't know. I just know he's got to go. That night I give him an overdose. That's that."

"Except", volunteered George Heap, studying his nails, "for our mutual – er – friend, Bentley."

"Wait for it," said Tabora irritably. Like all showmen, he resented interruption. "I get Roarer stuffed. Already Bentley's talking about postmortems. I blow. I'm through and I know it. I've got a couple of thousand iron men in the bank. I plan to lie low and let the thing fade out. Just as I'm getting around to it, I look out of my window one day and who do I see?"

"Bentley."

Tabora slapped the barrel. "Look," he barked, "will you keep out of this? My story, isn't it?"

"My apologies. Please continue."

"Yep. Bentley. I shadow him all that day. That night he heads for the Chandor dump. Right outside my door I breeze up to him and tell him O.K., I'll split even with the insurance claim if he'll keep his goddam mouth shut." He laughed shortly. "He fell for it. He must have thought it stank, but he couldn't resist it. We went up to my room. Well, who loses his nerve this time?"

131

George Heap said nothing.

"Bentley," said Tabora. "He shakes like a jelly. He says he doesn't want *my* dough, he's after your niece. He comes across with the stuff about your Mom." He saw George Heap stiffen and added hastily. "No offence. But the spiel about the axe gives me an idea. I fetch the axe and test out this idea. It works."

George Heap nodded. "You have perhaps some smattering of medical knowledge?"

"You want to hear this story – or do you?"

"Certainly."

"Well, *shuddup!* I get him downstairs, ease him over the wall, toss over the axe. Next moment I'm in the saloon with my alibi? How's that?" he paused.

"Do you want me to comment?" asked George Heap.

Tabora nodded. He expected praise. Praise was different.

George Heap studied his signet ring. In his opinion, the crime was unpardonable. It was brutish, chancy, lacking flair to a marked degree. "May I inquir,e" he said, "why you turned upon Miss Tossit?"

Tabora was so eager to tell his story that he did not notice the omission. "She started yapping about the axe. Then she says she never saw my friend leave. I know as soon as she hears Bentley's missing, she's going to start doing whatever she does instead of thinking." He stopped and looked up. "Say, where *is* that dame?"

"I have her. Please continue."

"You? Is it *you* that keeps snatching my stiffs?"

"I or members of my family."

"Ah," said Tabora. "I wondered about that."

"There is no need for anxiety."

"She was trash," said Tabora. "She got in my hair."

George Heap dunked his cigar in the beer. "You are in a difficult position, Mr. Tabora. Miss Tossit is at present in the back of my car. If you should be so foolhardy as to murder me, she will undoubtedly be found."

"Can it, gramp," said Tabora. He stood up, "You leave here feet first."

George Heap, too, stood up. He did not answer immediately. He took off his scarf and ran it through his hands. He tied it casually into the Studdingsail Halyard Bend. "You taught me this," he observed.

"What of it?" snarled Tabora. He swung an arm, limbering up.

"As it happens, I too am no novice." George Heap's eye fell on the gardenia. He picked it up, shook the beer from it, and replaced it in his buttonhole.

"So?" Tabora laughed.

George Heap frowned. "It is a matter of indifference to me, whether you believe me or not. If you will step over here, I will endeavor to break your neck."

Tabora sneered. "Come off it, gramp!" He twiddled the axe. "You haven't a chance."

George Heap concealed a smile. "Wait," he said. "How will the survivor explain the other's mutilated body? Shall we both write suicide notes?"

"Quite a comic," said Tabora. "Self defense is my story. You attack me. You fall. You bump your head. Won't be no axe when the cops show up."

"I see." The Strangler considered. "Very well. The explanation shall be mutual. In my case, it is slightly implausible, but if you insist upon this rodeo ..."

"I got to hand it to you, gramp," said Tabora. "You got guts." He laughed confidently.

George Heap thought briefly of his first victim. The man had had biceps like ostrich eggs; he too had been overconfident, under-intelligent. He stretched the scarf between his hands. He knew that he was at a disadvantage physically. It did not dismay him. The Heaps were natural killers. It was in the ... in the breed.

Tabora did not intend to hit the old man with the blade. He turned the axe over in his hands.

George Heap shot his cuffs. "Would you not feel more at home," he asked politely, "with a chair in your hands?"

"Shuddup!" roared Tabora. He raised the axe.

George Heap flirted the scarf, an insolent, matador gesture.

Tabora sprang.

George Heap turned his wrist. The scarf flicked the candle into the beer.

## CHAPTER 19

" 'ALF o'mild," said the butcher's second string.

Mrs. Filby jerked at the brass handle. The nozzle coughed. Two drops fell. Mrs. Filby frowned. She glanced at Mr. Tooley. She did not want to send him down to the cellar. He had had quite enough already. True, he was now drinking ginger ale, but he was far from sober. He was humming tonelessly to himself, performing some sort of soft shoe shuffle around

133

the corner where he imagined that she could not see him. Mrs. Filby filled the butcher's glass surreptitiously from the drip pan and decided to go down herself. She slid the glass across the counter and went out into the passage. She took a piece of chalk and drew a large circle around Mr. Tooley on the ground.

"You stay in there," she ordered.

Mr. Tooley took no notice of her.

Mossop was lying in his basket in the kitchen, a tired old cat. He looked at Mrs. Filby and yawned. The cellar door did not budge. The key had been removed. Mrs. Filby marched back to Mr. Tooley and went systematically through his pockets. He went on shuffling about, apparently oblivious of her presence.

She went back to the cellar door and peered through the keyhole. She could see nothing. She was going through her own pockets when she distinctly heard a dull thud from the cellar. She bent again, listening intently. A crash, then somebody running up the stairs. Mr. Tooley was prancing about behind her.

"Be quiet," she said over her shoulder.

Mr. Tooley froze. "Be quiet," he repeated. Then, in a sudden shout, "*Be quiet!*"

Hugh came around the corner of the passage. "What's going on?" he asked.

Sukie appeared behind him. "Where's Uncle George?" she demanded.

Mr. Scales trotted up behind her. He stood holding his hat in both hands looking puzzled.

Mrs. Filby thumped on the cellar door. An answering thump came from the inside. Alistair and Miss Dogtinder appeared together. Miss Dogtinder was still clutching her drink.

"What's happening?" asked Alistair.

"What's cooking?" snapped Miss Dogtinder.

A weak thud from inside the cellar.

"Fetch the police," said a breathless, unrecognizable voice through the keyhole. "There's going to be an accident!" Another crash, a series of bumps.

"Who's that?" shouted Hugh. "What's going on there?"

"*Fetch the police!*"

Mrs. Filby turned on Sukie. "You sure they've …?" she began. She saw Mr. Scales watching her. "Oo's down there?" she asked meaningly.

Sukie nodded reassuringly. "Nobody we know," she said.

"It must be Uncle George."

"All right then. Fetch Albert."

"Force the door!" said Hugh.

"Where's Beecher?"

"*Beecher!*"

"Beecher!" roared Mr. Tooley from his circle. "Into the breacher, Beecher!" He fell down laughing.

A muffled shout from the cellar. "Help! *Murder!*"

"That's Uncle George!" said Sukie faintly. She hurled herself against the door.

"Get the axe!" shouted Hugh.

Alistair rushed into the kitchen. Hugh lunged against the cellar door. Sukie ran to fetch Beecher. She found him in the saloon. He was empty-ing the contents of the stocking for the blind babies of Battersea into a handkerchief. Sukie tugged at his arm. She dragged him into the passage. Miss Dogtinder was standing at the telephone, tapping a long foot. "Of-ficer," she was saying. "Is that you, officer?"

Mr. Scales stood aside to let Beecher pass. He touched Sukie's elbow. "What's it all about?" he asked. "I don't understand."

"Gangway!" called Sukie. "Gangway for Beecher!"

The group around the cellar door fell back. Hugh was chopping at the door with the axe. Beecher pushed him aside and went down on one knee. He looked over his shoulder at the circle of anxious faces.

" 'Ere!" he said. "You don't watch me. Turn round!"

"Help!" came a faint, despairing shout from the cellar. It was followed by a grinding crash.

Beecher produced a bent nail, a piece of iron wire, and a penknife.

"Hurry, hurry, hurry!" said Sukie wildly.

Miss Dogtinder tapped her on the shoulder. "I have summoned the boys in blue," she announced. "They were reluctant to believe me. I trust that this is not another wild goose chase. If so, I shall appear a veritable damn fool."

Beecher fiddled delicately. His heavy face was somber. He was com-pletely absorbed. Sukie crouched beside him, trying to see under the door. On the far side there was an oath and a loud splash. Then complete si-lence.

Sukie sat back on her heels. "He's killed him!" she whispered. "He's dead."

There was a faint tinkle as the key fell out of the lock on the far side. The door opened half an inch. Beecher stood up. "I never been 'ere," he growled. "I don't know none o' you, an' I can prove it."

He pushed past Miles and ran along the passage. Mr. Tooley was lying on the ground inside the circle of chalk, drinking from a ginger-ale bottle.

135

Beecher leapt over him, shot through the saloon, and out into the mews.

It was raining, a misty drizzle. Beecher's boots clattered on the cobbles. Halfway down, he heard the siren. He vaulted over the palings on to the bomb site. He sprang through a shattered window. A few bricks fell. The police car skidded to a stop at the top of the mews. Two large men in mackintoshes leapt out and rushed into Miss Dogtinder's house.

A constable appeared at the end of the road. Another rode down Tite Street on a bicycle. The two detectives came out of Miss Dogtinder's house. One of them rang the Chandors' bell. The other prowled around George Heap's drophead coupé. He measured the distance between the front wheel and the pavement and wrote something in his notebook. He walked around to the back of the car and noted the number. The first detective backed into the road and looked up at the Chandors' windows. Stepping over the fence, he rang Miles' bell. The constable on the bicycle rode down Wharf Mews. The second detective was drumming his fingers on the trunk on the back of George Heap's car.

Beecher, crouching among Miss Dogtinder's tomato plants, clutched his face. The mere sight of the hurry-up wagon made him shudder. He knew that if he were picked up now it would mean at least ten years in the Flowery! He bit the back of his hand.

The second detective was bending closer to look at the trunk. He was examining the lock. He said something to his companion. The other man jumped over Miles' fence and joined him. One straightened up and blew a whistle. The constable on foot ran towards them.

Beecher bounded through a crumbling house and ducked behind a tree. Joan was there, rubbing her damp hindquarters against the lower boughs. Beecher jerked her out of the way. He peered around the tree. The detectives had the trunk on the ground now. They were bending over it, touching it gingerly, trying to open it.

The constable came running out of the Carp. He shouted. The first detective said something to the other man and ran down the mews towards the public house. The second detective jumped into the police car and grabbed the mobile telephone.

They were bringing up reinforcements! Beecher's heart beat faster. This was no place for a screwsman. The only place he wanted to be at the moment was back in his own Toby, reestablishing his alibi.

He forced his way through a clump of goldenrod, ran bent double across an overgrown lawn, sprang over a wall. He lowered himself off another wall and with his special run, which looked at a distance like a walk, he raced up Tite Street towards the haven of King's Road.

The door creaked as Hugh lunged against it. Alistair stopped biting his nails and sprang to help him. Miles Tate-Grahame and Mr. Scales stood silently side by side, staring. Mrs. Filby was clutching Mossop, Miss Dogtinder was tearing her jabot to shreds.

Sukie ran out of the kitchen with a torch. Hugh and Alistair hurled themselves again at the door. It wheezed, then swung slowly inwards.

Alistair and Hugh fell back, panting. For a moment nobody moved. The stairs descended into pitch darkness. There was complete silence.

"They're dead," said Sukie. "They're both dead."

Hugh took the torch from her and directed its beam into the darkness. "Hullo!" he called. "Is there anybody there?" His voice broke. He cleared his throat and tried once again.

There was a faint splashing at the bottom of the stairs. Sukie was conscious of Miss Dogtinder's face behind her shoulder. She could hear the woman breathing. She started downstairs. Hugh snatched her by the arm and pulled her back. He dropped the torch. It rolled down the stairs, bouncing from step to step.

There was an exclamation from the darkness. Somebody was coming upstairs, walking very slowly. His shoes squelched. Hugh pushed Sukie behind him. Alistair dodged behind Miss Dogtinder. A faint smell of beer and spirits rose from the cellar. A man appeared dimly. He was bending over, brushing at his trousers. He came up the last three stairs and stood at the top blinking. It was George Heap.

His feet were wet, the gardenia was hanging from his buttonhole, a scarf was tied around his neck in the Magnus Hitch, but otherwise he looked his normal self. He was attending to his hair with a pocket comb. He adjusted his tie and smiled faintly.

"I'm afraid that there has been an accident," he murmured.

Hugh moved first. He pushed past the Strangler and raced down the dark stairs. At the bottom he splashed into the beer. He struck a match and stared. A fine spray was still squirting from one of the barrels. Two others were overturned. A broken trestle poked out of the scummy flood. There was a pile of broken bottles, a shelf torn loose, a chunk of plaster fallen from the ceiling. The match went out. Hugh struck another and saw Tabora at once. He bent to feel the man's pulse. The lion tamer was dead. He had been hit on the head with something blunt.

Hugh turned and ran upstairs. The passage was full of policemen. Everybody was talking at once. There was a tall man in a mackintosh holding a pair of handcuffs. Miss Dogtinder had fainted. A constable was pushing her out of the way. The butcher's second string was standing on a crate behind the policemen. He looked at Hugh and said, "Cor!" Sukie was saying over and over again, "Where's Albert? We asked for *Albert*."

137

Hugh saw George Heap in the kitchen. He went in and shut the door behind him. The Strangler was washing his hands in the sink.

Hugh stopped. He intended to speak but he did not know what to say. He cleared his throat.

George Heap looked around for a towel. "He attempted to strangle me," he said. "The beggar! The insolence!"

"I'm afraid there's going to be trouble."

"Oh yes," said George Heap indifferently. He smiled. "I repaid him in kind. I smote him with his own discarded weapon."

Mrs. Filby rushed into the kitchen, filled a glass with water, and rushed out again.

"Where's Albert?" insisted Sukie above the babble of voices in the passage.

Hugh stood in the middle of the kitchen. "I may be able to get you off on a manslaughter charge."

George Heap frowned. "You will do no such thing," he said sharply. "Kindly inform your army of incompetents that I shall require no reference in court to the insane fiesta of the past few days. I do not wish my trial to degenerate into an *opéra bouffe*."

"*Where's Albert?*"

"Constable Chivvers?" inquired a cultured voice. "He is at home with a slight chill. Is there anybody here by the name of George Heap?"

The Strangler looked at Hugh. His eyes sparkled. He lit a cigar and strolled into the passage. The circle of faces turned towards him.

George Heap bowed slightly towards the tall man in the mackintosh. He touched his mustache with the tip of a finger.

"Inspector Stoner, I presume?" he said.

## CHAPTER 20

FIVE months had passed.

George Heap poured a cup of coffee. The tailor waited patiently with a needle in his mouth and a square of blue chalk in one hand. He screwed up his eyes and squinted at the Strangler's trousers.

"Honestly, old chap," said Tribling. "A rotten experience! I am thankful for you that it is all over. I'm afraid that you have suffered considerable inconvenience."

George Heap patted the ash off his cigar. "Steward!" he called, "A cigar for Mr. Tribling." He went on without a pause, "The trial was unreasonably impressive, was it not?"

Tribling coughed, "Your exchange with Stoner was most entertaining."

"The jacket, sir, if you please," said the tailor. George Heap put it on. "Beautiful cloth, sir. Shrunk by Macwindus and Cornham. It has only just been released for the home market."

Tribling looked at it admiringly. "Ought to wear well," he remarked, snuffling into his handkerchief. He still had his cold.

George Heap smiled. "That, my dear fellow, is why I selected it." He pulled impatiently at the lapel. "This drape is too tropical."

"I see the trouble, sir," said the tailor. He laid hold of the shoulder and with a convulsive movement ripped off the sleeve. "If you will raise the arm, sir."

George Heap raised his arm. "In your opinion, Tribling, was the verdict a popular one?"

Tribling nodded several times. "I think so," he said. "By and large."

George Heap laughed shortly. "My counsel — would you credit it? — was at first inclined to plead guilty but insane! It was only after a regrettable display of physical force that he was persuaded to suppress certain witnesses whose testimony might have contributed to that end."

Tribling was embarrassed. He blew his nose violently. "Absurd!" he said. Suddenly doubtful, he added slyly, "Were *you* satisfied, old man?"

George Heap's eyelids drooped. "Obviously," he said.

The tailor darted behind him and snatched the collar off his jacket. There was a moment of silence. The tailor fell on his knees and plunged his hand up the back of the Strangler's waistcoat. He got hold of something inside and jerked at it. George Heap sipped his brandy.

"You dined well?" inquired Tribling.

"Very indifferently. *Tinned* orange with the duck! The crêpe suzette was emulsive. I distinctly ordered a Clos de Vougeot '29 and was fobbed off with a Pommard '34." He sighed. "Times have changed, Tribling. Times have indeed changed." He turned upon the tailor. "Can you account for this crippled effect upon the right hip?"

The tailor reared upwards. "It's the tackin'," he snapped, suddenly aggressive. He grabbed off the other sleeve and put it in his pocket.

Tribling noted his friend's expression. "I say," he said quickly. "Do you think I could have a cup of coffee?"

George Heap tore his eyes from the tailor's trachea. He poured the coffee, sugared it, and carried it across to Tribling. He stood still, gnawing his lip.

"Lately," he murmured, closing his eyes, "I have been almost continually frustrated. It is of course quite absurd, but I'm afraid that the cup will not go through the bars."

Hugh walked down Wharf Mews whistling. The cobbles were still wet and shining after an April shower. The weeds had sprung up on the bomb site. A pink cherry and a lilac were in bloom. Senator was standing in the long grass swishing his tail. Beside him, with only the tips of her horns visible, was the goat. Behind them, the far side of a tangle of briars, was Miss Dogtinder. She was in the middle of her flourishing allotment, pulling up carrots. Hugh looked at her curiously. It was hard to believe that less than four months ago she had been fined for contempt of court; that she had caused laughter in the gallery by demanding of the prosecuting counsel the date of his birth; that she had made headlines by rebuking the judge for wearing scarlet on a Tuesday.

He crossed the mews. He noticed that the poster on the hoarding had been changed again. It now showed Dorothy Lamour sitting in a canoe with a monkey around her neck. The goat had not yet discovered it. Hugh smiled and walked a little faster. He had brought back his wig to show Sukie. He changed his dispatch case to the other hand and dropped a brief.

It was cool and dim in the saloon bar after the thin spring sunlight. There was a vase of daffodils on the mantelpiece. Sukie had not yet arrived. From the Ladies' Bar came the enthusiastic voices of Mae, Lil, and Doris. They were discussing Mae's new whitlow.

Mrs. Filby was behind the bar humming snatches from *The Maid of the Mountains*. There had been a real danger during the sensational weeks of the trial that she would be transferred to a State-controlled House. That morning's post had brought her reprieve. Mr. Tooley was capering about behind her. He was drinking ginger ale. He threw a bag of potato crisps happily into the air and failed to catch them.

Mr. Scales was standing quietly by the counter fingering some new hardwood samples. He measured Mr. Tooley with his eye. *Standard six-foot waxed yew*, he thought.

"Drink?" Miles Tate-Grahame asked Alistair. "As if I didn't know."

"Now there's a point," said Alistair brightly. "Bitter please."

"Lost the taste for gin-and-French?" inquired Mrs. Filby mildly.

Alistair did not blush but his ears moved. "A lot of water has flowed into your beer since then," he said coldly. "You used to take paying guests."

"An amazing affair," said Miles, shaking his long gray head. "Of course the man was insane. In my opinion, many cases of maniac elation can be traced directly back to the bed-sitting-room. The gas ring has the most appalling subconscious associations. Jung ..."

" 'E's off," said Mrs. Filby. She went down to the far end of the bar and began to whisper to the butcher's second string about gammon.

Sukie came in. She hurried across to Hugh and took his arm. "Hullo, darling," she said, "I've just had another anonymous postcard from Beecher. He's in Joe Gurr again. He got nicked in Cardiff on a snout gaff. Doesn't seem to care much. It's only a two stretch and a lot of the Boys had their collars felt at about the same time." She ordered herself a ginger beer and carried it across into a corner. "Darling?"

"Mm?"

"Uncle George *wasn't*, you know."

Hugh said nothing.

"It was proved, wasn't it? Mummy was afraid that he'd wind up with her. They never got on well. I'm so glad that he's right next to Granny. They make such a distinguished couple. Do you know that Mr. Tribling goes there twice a week and gives Uncle George a fresh gardenia?"

"He was a beneficiary under the will."

"He only got a collection of old scarves." She shook the ginger beer in her glass. "Uncle George told me in strict confidence that he'd killed four other people but he'd never even set eye on Marigold Tossit."

"He pleaded guilty."

"Well, there wasn't much alternative, was there? I mean, everybody knew that he'd conked Tabora and there was Marigold in the back of the car killed in exactly the same way ... It's a bit strong, isn't it?"

"He killed them all right."

"He said not. He said he had an alibi. He was making a sentimental journey to the scene of his first crime. He didn't want to tell them that. He thought it would confuse them."

"Who did he say he'd killed?"

"He said he was the Strangler."

"Nonsense! Tabora was the Strangler. He tried to strangle Uncle George. The scarf was tied in the Magnus Hitch like all the other cases."

"Uncle George told me in confidence that it was *his* scarf. They got their weapons mixed up banging about in the dark. I'd hate to be a police-man, wouldn't you? Very muddling."

"Inspector Stoner's father went to Eton."

"Uncle George said that explained everything. He didn't seem to ... *mind*, did he? He said that he'd outwitted them to the last. He told me not to tell anybody because the joke was too exquisite to be bandied about by the general public."

"Let's face it, love. He must have been a bit ..."

"And I say that he was *not*. You've only got to look at him in the Chamber of Horrors. He looks beautiful. That nice suit and everything."

"There's a wrinkle on the left hip."

"The tailor was late for the last fitting. *Too* late." She hesitated. "Darling?"

"What?"

"You never truly believed that it was me, did you?"

"No," said Hugh firmly. "What nonsense," he added.

Sukie beamed. "Yes, isn't it?" she said. "I just *couldn't* do a thing like that, not in cold blood."

A small man in a blue overcoat came in. Mossop sprang off the Guinness barrel and sneaked into the passage. The regulars watched the man uneasily. Was he a reporter, a policeman, or just another nosey parker? They had been through a trying time during the past months. At the sight of an unknown face, a deep silence fell throughout the House.

The little man went over to the counter and ordered himself a Guinness. Mrs. Filby drew it, watching him in the mirror. Mr. Tooley stood behind her with his mouth open.

The stranger produced a stubby thermometer and dipped it into the stout. Mr. Tooley's tiny eyes narrowed. For the first time in thirty years a slow blush crept up Mrs. Filby's neck.

" 'Ere," said the man quietly. "I'll 'ave to make a report. This gorgeous liquid is nine degrees too 'ot."

## THE END

>>> If you've enjoyed this book and would like to discover more great vintage crime and thriller titles, as well as the most exciting crime and thriller authors writing today, visit: >>>

## The Murder Room
### Where Criminal Minds Meet

**themurderroom.com**

>>>

www.ingramcontent.com/pod-product-compliance
Ingram Content Group UK Ltd.
Pitfield, Milton Keynes, MK11 3LW, UK
UKHW022308280225
455674UK00004B/219

9 781471 912283